RUFUS STEELE: 1938

To Jill and Frank —

Susan C. Turner

RUFUS STEELE: 1938

Susan C. Turner

Harry Douglas Press
Tampa, FL

This book is a work of fiction. Any references to historical events or real people are used fictitiously. Any resemblance to actual persons or events is entirely coincidental.

Harry Douglas Press
704 West Swann Avenue
Tampa, FL 33606

First Harry Douglas Press paperback edition, April 2009

Text copyright ©2009 by Susan C. Turner

All rights reserved, including the right of reproduction in whole or in part except in the case of brief quotations embodied in critical articles and reviews.

Printed in the United States of America.

The text of this book was set in 14-point Adobe Garamond Pro.

Cover and book design by 1106 Design, LLC

Library of Congress Control Number: 2009900616

ISBN-13: 978-0-9822842-0-9

Summary: In the small farming community of Friendsville, Maryland in 1938, fourteen-year-old Henry Murphy and his brothers work hard and sometimes fight for their lives. Mysterious and courageous, Dr. Rufus Steele proves to be a powerful ally, and strong bonds develop amidst dangerous circumstances.

For my father, Warren,
and his brothers Arthur, Stanley (Jim),
Glen (Bill), Ivan, Orval, June, and Ken

*"A stranger I arrived here.
A stranger I go hence."*

—*Winterreise Gute Nacht,*
Wilhelm Muller

Chapter One

"And he's contagious," warned Dr. Steele. "Keep him away from the rest of the family. Make sure he drinks lots of water and gets plenty of rest; chicken broth for breakfast, lunch and dinner, and a cup of your hot ginger tea at bedtime. In about an hour, send Henry down to the drugstore to pick up the boy's medication. I'll stop when I get to town and talk to Ray McConnell about it. Let me know if there's any change."

With those words, Rufus Steele turned from my mother's worried face and stared hard into the brown bare field beyond our front steps. I'd seen that look before—a mixture of pain and resolve—and hoped it had nothing to do with my kid brother Jim's feverish condition. Yesterday, Jim arrived home after school, red-faced and burning hot, flung himself across our shared bed and slept through supper—an infrequent occurrence at our house, especially for Jim. When he awoke this morning in the same sorry state, my mother sent me hurrying to town to fetch Dr. Steele.

Rufus Steele was rightly named—a solid man, a sharp doctor. Lately, our small community, my own family included, had seen difficult times, and Rufus Steele had become a significant presence.

I followed his eyes toward the distant gray ridge, but was hard pressed to follow his thoughts. Over the past few months, I'd wondered a lot about Rufus Steele. Where had he spent the first years of his life, and what magnet had brought him here? Medical school graduates generally steered clear of rural farming towns in the Allegheny Mountains, especially in 1938. Dr. Glenn Gard, our most recent town doctor, died two years ago in a house fire while his wife and young daughter visited relatives in Kentucky. Folks around here speculated he'd fallen asleep in front of a blazing hearth that quickly engulfed the first floor. After that tragic event, families traveled the twenty miles to Grantsville if they needed serious medical tending.

As I recall, I'd been to a doctor only once. When my mother couldn't remedy away a boil on my stomach, she, carrying a basket of eggs and a tub of her creamiest butter, reluctantly walked me into Dr. Gard's office. Using a sharp knife and three quick strokes, the ugly mess was lanced, drained, and bandaged. It hurt pretty bad for about a week. In a good light, I can still see the white scar on my right side.

I remember the day Rufus Steele arrived—third Tuesday of last May. Noticed him the second he climbed out of that scuffed-up green Model A Ford Coupe. He was wearing an odd gray hat, broad-brimmed in front and shortened in back, unusual for these parts. With his right hand, he'd adjusted the brim against the morning sun, pulling it down tight against his forehead, then dropped the car key in his pocket and took a slow deep breath of mountain air, stretching his arms full length toward the clear blue sky. Standing directly across from him on Maple Street, headed west on my way to school, I slowed my pace a bit so as to get a good look at the man who'd parked his old car squarely in front of my father's general store.

Of late, I amused myself by observing strangers' movements and attaching some importance of character to their outward appearance. Unfortunately, I seldom had cause to do so, as I pretty much knew everyone in town—and they me—for my entire life. On occasion, I would spot an unfamiliar miner or railroad worker in town and set to assigning them an imaginary personal history. This particular stranger presented the perfect practice opportunity: slim but well fed, slightly taller and straighter than my father, clean-shaven, light close-cropped hair under that hat. Age, hard to tell, but I guessed in the range of thirty to thirty-five. His clothes and the casual nature of his stance led me to believe he was an outdoor sort, or at least comfortable stalking through piney woods with a rabbit hound at his heels. While not secure about judging a man's handsomeness, I knew my Aunt Carol would find him worth a second, or third, look. The same feeling told me he was not a married man.

Of course, I could not observe on that first morning the part of Rufus Steele I'll never forget, the part I cherish most. His voice, then and now, is like no other to me.

But I'm getting way ahead of myself.

That first morning, I angled down the road still staring in his direction, and he fixed me with a gaze, a brief smile, and a touch to his gray hat. I thought momentarily about where such a man might come from and what he could be doing in our small town. But by the time I limped through the schoolyard gate, I was thinking more about an explanation for my missing algebra homework and the blister on my right heel. Ray Kiser, my ninth grade math teacher, assigned two pages of homework each and every night. Usually, I knuckled down and put in the time to get them done. Today, Mr. Kiser would be disappointed in his prized student. Much as I tried to talk myself out of taking responsibility for the missing papers, I knew my own lack of effort (and resistance to pain) were to blame.

Yesterday after my afternoon shift, I left my homework sheets under the cash register counter and decided not to make the difficult trudge back to town to retrieve them. In any case, I knew there wasn't much point in asking for either a pardon or an extension. Mr. Kiser made that message clear on the first and every subsequent day of class. I saw two zeros in my future.

The stranger did not enter my mind again until I spied, on the trip from school to store, that old Ford parked between Selby's Service Station and Fox's Feed Store. In the front seat, two men sat engaged in serious conversation passing papers back and forth. The late spring afternoon sun shone strongly on the windshield so I couldn't make out their identities as I ambled by. But I assumed the stranger in the gray hat to be one of them.

The following day, I (and most of the town's population) learned that a man named Rufus Steele had bought the single-story burned-out brick structure on the southeast corner of Maple Street and Third Avenue. Bud Sykes, Friendsville's only licensed real estate agent, spent a good long hour in the general store telling the whole transaction—in fine detail, start to finish—to my father and the regulars who sat, or leaned, around the black coal stove in the middle of the floor.

From sun up to sundown over the next month, sounds of scraping and pounding and sawing emanated from that house across the street from our store, though we never saw anyone except a wiry black cat coming or going. Conversations about the summer weather and whose barn needed repair gave way to reckonings and re-reckonings about the cause and outcome of all that activity.

During these discussions, I always kept one eye on Hiram Savage. Hiram possessed a keen sense of balance. I pondered frequently on how he managed to prop one foot against the base of the old stove, swing the other leg slowly back and forth, stare at the ceiling, and remain upright on one back chair leg.

By the end of June, the construction noise came to an end. The red brick house had been rebuilt and remodeled to combine a simple home and office. One morning we noted a black cat with white whiskers sitting in its front window and a square brass sign on a sturdy wooden frame near the road:

Family Medicine
Rufus Steele, M.D.
152 Maple Street

During the first few weeks in July, Dr. Steele taught himself the current condition of the town's health and handled the occasional emergency (like the afternoon my classmate Cecil Gross missed a copperhead and shot his uncle in the lower thigh with his 22). By day, Dr. Steele spent time at Ray McConnell's drug store, conversing with its owner about medicines, items that people in town needed and what they bought at the store. Two Saturday mornings I recognized his gray hat at the town shooting match. On a rainy afternoon at the end of July as I peered out the general store's front door, I saw him cross the street heading to Fox's Feed Store. I figured, since Dr. Steele had no livestock to feed, that he was registering to vote.

While Dr. Steele was learning a great deal about all of us, however, we knew virtually nothing about him—except that he was a registered Democrat and couldn't hit a bull's-eye target.

Chapter Two

The green Model A Coupe pulled slowly to the curb and stopped. Its owner opened the door and stepped out onto the running board, then hopped down onto the street.

"Mornin', Henry."

"You know me?" I questioned.

The man nodded and stuck out his hand. "Know your name's Henry Murphy, first person I set eyes on when I arrived in Friendsville. Your father owns Murphy's General Store across the road from my place. We haven't met. I'm Dr. Steele."

Unaccustomed to formal introductions, I stared at the outstretched hand, unsure of his intent. Some notion told me to put out my hand, too, and we shook firmly. His powerful hand was larger than my own, but I judged that I managed a good enough squeeze.

"Don't mean to take up your time," Dr. Steele said, "but I wondered if you might show me around town—at your convenience."

"W-w-what do you mean?" I stammered.

"I'd like to walk around, learn some local history. Would you mind?"

My first reaction to his request no doubt registered plainly on my face. He waited me out as I struggled for the words to explain both the town's suspicions and my own physical pain.

"I don't rightly know what I could help you with that you don't already know about all of us in town, and my foot's not feeling too well for a whole lot of walking," I sputtered.

"Maybe I could take a look at that foot for you," Dr. Steele offered.

"Thanks, but my mother does all the doctoring in our house," I replied too quickly.

"I couldn't help but notice you've been limping on that foot for quite awhile, Henry, and I imagine it hurts a little, too."

"Not much," I lied.

"All the same, I'm concerned about it," Dr. Steele insisted. "Can I give you a lift home?"

I hesitated only a minute before nodding enthusiastically and climbing through the passenger door. Home was more than a mile away. My heel throbbed in spite of my recent assurance, and I couldn't see missing the opportunity to ride in a car like that Ford Coupe. For the next quarter hour I greedily sniffed the leather upholstery and surveyed the knobs and dials along the dashboard while I respectfully fielded Dr. Steele's questions about the town, the river, and the trees that lined Maple Street. Before we reached our farmhouse, I reckoned I'd provided him a pretty fair summary of our town's past and present conditions without giving away too much in the telling.

As local legend goes, the town of Friendsville owes its beginnings to John Friend and his wife Karrennhappuck who traded an iron pot and a collection of household goods to a branch of the Shawnee Indians in exchange for a piece of land along the Youghiogheny River. In 1763, Friend built a cabin on the river. Over the next 175 years, coal, timber, farming, and the B & O Railroad increased the town's population to more than 800—enough to allow my father and the rest of the Maple Street merchants to eke out a living nearly sufficient to support their families.

A garden plot, a few cows in the barn, a hog pen, and a good hunting rifle provide most families with three meals a day and a full smokehouse for the winter. We never knew anyone in town to go hungry, and we all worked hard to provide. When I was eight, my father taught me the proper way to shoot squirrels and rabbits. Since then, I'm always careful to aim for the head so as not to ruin any of the meat.

Many families suffer through harsh winters that may start as early as mid-September when the first snows cover and freeze the ground. After the first big snowfall, my father retrieves the snow shovels from the woodhouse and places them beside the back door. My hands never warm from shoveling a path to the barn twice a day to feed and milk the cows. I often wonder if those cows know their daily hay comes at the cost of my brother Jim's and my own frozen fingers and toes.

Most likely, we won't see the ground again until May Day. Throughout the fall, winter, and early spring, our furnace puts out irregular blasts of heat—as long as our coal supply lasts.

"Guess I ought to be thinking about heat for the winter, too," said Dr. Steele. "Where would I get a load of coal?"

I knew our family coal came from a vein shaft in the mountain up above our house. My father and my Uncle Frank's two boys, Woodrow and Glenn, dug it out two years ago. But we harvest just enough from that small vein to make it through our own winter.

"I were you, I'd take a ride over to Vindex. Talk to the mining company there," I replied.

As we bumped up the dirt road over the last hill past Nolan Kendall's small store, I hoped Imogene

Kendall was busy with a customer. For some reason, I didn't want anyone thinking the new doctor was a friend of mine.

Chapter Three

I folded the church bulletin into my back pocket, and Jim and I set off down the road. Jim hugged the left ditch searching for the last wild blueberries of September while I strayed toward the middle hoping to find the smoothest plane for my ailing heel. Every few days, my mother soaked and dressed the angry spot and imagined it improving. But I knew different. Walking was painful, and I was more and more aware of my foot's placement, even on the flattest surface. In fact, I spent way too much time planning ahead for each movement, so as to cause the least amount of hurt. Increasingly, I recalled the new doctor's offer, but loyalty to my mother's care prevailed. I could abide a little pain. There are plenty of boys my age who have worse.

My parents drive home from Sunday services in our old Model T, but Jim and I prefer to take the shortcut through the white pines my father planted years ago. Birds perch and hide in the dense needles that provide shelter for squirrels and other small animals. The trees' angled light reminds me of some heavenly force, particularly after a reproachful sermon by the preacher. This specific morning, my father warned us to keep our eyes open for any wayward bears and steer clear of them. While he did not elaborate on this caution, I'd overheard a conversation at the general store regarding suspicion of a rabid animal in the mountains above Bear Creek. I kept my better eye on Jim as I knew that bears favored blueberries as much as he did, especially at this time of year.

Friendsville's surrounding forests provide the perfect home for black bears, and we come across our share of sows and boars during the summer and fall months when berries and beechnuts are plentiful. They usually forage during the early morning and at twilight when the heat lessens. Generally, bears are afraid of humans, and so long as they see an escape route, they move on. No telling what a rabid bear might do, though.

We arrived at our farmhouse just as the preacher pulled in. After services, Seven Springs Church members customarily invite the preacher and his wife to dinner. My mother's thick butter noodles and freshly-baked pies make them more regular visitors at our table than any other. I gazed hungrily down at the broad plank table dressed in white cloth and overloaded with covered dishes. Is there anything better than the smell of roasted chicken and fresh butter beans? Two fresh pies, the end result for the blackberries Jim and I picked yesterday morning, waited in the pantry pie safe. The sun's placement in the sky and the cooling air led me to ponder that today might be the year's last outdoor Sunday dinner.

Sunday is my father's only day of rest. In addition to owning and working the general store, he cuts timber for the lumber mill, and plows and plants and tends our 20 acres of corn, potatoes and pole beans. At harvest time, he closes the store to join a dozen farmers for the two weeks it takes to move from farm to farm to bring in everyone's oats and wheat. Lester Robey owns the threshing machine and tractor used for the harvest. Lester runs the thresher for all the farms on our mountain. With our neighbors working behind him, Lester's machines thresh the crops on every planted acre. At midday, after a full morning of labor, the men break for a huge noon meal prepared by their wives and daughters and brought out to the field where they're working.

This year, I was expected to contribute my share of labor, and I had been excused from school for that sole purpose. While I liked school and proved a steady and able student (much to my mother's pride), I looked forward to my first year of fall harvesting that would begin tomorrow morning.

I was well prepared for harvesting chores. I spent the summer preceding my fourteenth birthday working over at Clyde Glover's farm near Accident. As his farm was much bigger than our own, Mr. Glover needed an extra hand, mostly for mending fences and feeding his cow herd. He showed up one morning to inquire whether my father would allow me to work for him.

"Andrew, would you consider letting one of your boys come out and work with me for the summer? I'll pay $15 a month with room and board."

I watched my father hesitate before scratching his lower lip and replying, "Clyde, you know my older boy, Stanley, works over in Selbysport now. You'll need to ask Henry if he's willing."

So long as the weather was good that summer, Arthur Glover (Clyde's older son) and I worked from four in the morning until the sun finally went down— well past eight o'clock. It was the first real money I ever earned. As a bonus, I learned to drive a rusty red pick-up truck all over the farm. Arthur, a pretty fair driver, preferred riding in the truck bed, so I figured we both made out pretty well on that deal. Once, on a rainy afternoon, Arthur, his sister Doris, and I drove the pick-up into Accident for a double-scoop ice cream cone. On the way home, I showed off my new driving skills for Doris. She seemed real impressed until I missed the turn-off road and ran us into a shallow ditch. We had a heck of a time pushing that truck back onto the road. Things only got worse when Doris discovered that her best dress resembled a well-used hog pen. My brother Jim was the only person who didn't make out too well that summer. For three months, he got stuck doing double chores. For his trouble, I handed him a couple dollars from my last pay.

"Finish your breakfast, Henry. Uncle Frank's on his way. And put those boots on before we go," directed my father as he buttoned up his flannel work shirt and grabbed his hat from the rack.

Coffee soup, a usual breakfast for Jim and me, consisted of sweet biscuits covered in coffee, sugar and milk. Finishing it was no trouble, but putting on my right boot proved a painful process. Tears stung my eyes as I wrenched it into place. I fixed my eyes on the floor to avoid my mother's careful gaze. Before she spoke, I thought she hadn't noticed me wiping my eyes on the corner of the tablecloth.

"It's time we saw the doctor about that heel, Henry. I'll see to it today while you're working," she said quietly.

My scrawny foot fit easily into Dr. Steele's hand. He waggled my toes, bent the ankle left and right, squeezed the arch, and then slowly lifted my outstretched leg to peer solemnly at my damaged heel. Lips puckered, eyes narrowed, the man sat staring and thinking a full minute. Since the examination began, no one had spoken. I thought it impolite to interrupt the silence. Tenderly, he tapped the hot red pulpy mass. I hardly recognized it as my own and sensed no feeling from his touch.

"You need something to halt this infection, Henry," he said as he painted my foot red with iodine. "And for the next week, you're to lie in bed with your foot propped up. This heel is in a bad way. Why did you wait so long to see me? I surely recall asking you about it the day I drove you home last month."

Without meeting my mother's eyes, I countered, "That foot's not too bad. It didn't hurt a bit until just this week."

Not one to allow her son to assume her obligation or to sustain a lie, my mother shot me a disapproving look as she pulled herself up and declared, "Dr. Steele, we're much obliged for your advice and your care. I reckon Henry's poor condition is as much my fault as any other. I've been nursing after that heel for more than three months now. It's long ago I should have noticed how far his health was damaged. We'll follow your direction."

Thus, on that chilly autumn evening, a mutual trust commenced between my mother, Martha Murphy, and Dr. Rufus Steele—a union they would put to use in the coming months. I, however, was still resistant and not so easily disposed to his confidence.

Chapter Four

My brother, Stanley, was as good a fur trapper as any mountain man. Every winter, he set his traps along the icy cold waters of Bear Creek hoping to snag gray and red fox, beaver, rabbit, and the occasional raccoon. When he accumulated an armload of pelts, he hitched a ride north to Uniontown where he sold them to a fur trader. In exchange for our help unloading the traps every day, Stanley put aside a few rabbit feet for Jim and me. When I was younger, I put more stock in possessing them than now. But Stanley enjoys the act of giving, so Jim's collection benefits from a small number of mine.

Stanley had taken a job driving a lumber truck up north of Selbysport which kept him away from home for the best part of the month. Lumbering is big business in Garrett County. Most weeks, Stanley managed to get home for Sunday dinner, but the remaining six days he drove heavy timber into Pittsburgh. It was not remarkable, then, for him to decide to place his traps early this year. The weather had turned cold in late October, and the ground soon would be frozen. The best pelts were harvested in late winter and early spring, and Stanley's traps could be used throughout the long winter. Late one Saturday afternoon, Stanley gathered his tools and prepared to set off on the two-mile hike to the creek. Jim and I begged to come along. After a half dozen smiling refusals, Stanley relented and allowed us to carry the heavy cast iron traps.

We walked carefully downhill toward Buffalo Creek through the bare field where wild strawberries grew into August, past our deserted swimming hole where Jim learned to swim and we all went skinny dipping last summer, and then followed a path to where Bear Creek crossed from the east. As we huffed along, the sun dropped lower in the sky, and the wind blew cooler on our faces. The beech trees rustled overhead. Three quarters of the way there, Stanley promised us a big gulp of fresh pure Bear Creek water when we reached our first destination. Jim and I both burst out as to how we preferred our mother's cool summer root beer. Just when the afternoon sun was hottest, she would appear suddenly at the top of the hill toting two big canning jars filled to the brim. We grinned at that delicious memory.

"Get ready with those traps. Up the path a piece we'll set the first one. You see these mounds here and droppings further along? Means a few muskrats live in this area. They're easy to catch. Got a bunch of 'em last year." Stanley dropped the tool pack from his shoulder and knelt down to survey the dirt. He moved closer to the creek bed and nodded as he saw the tracks he'd been looking for. "Right here. Let's have that number one double coil spring." As Jim handed over the first trap, Stanley unloaded a cleat and a foot-long plank from his pack, and secured the trap to the board. At an angle, he wedged the board into the creek bottom so that the trap was hidden in the water. He fished a fat green apple out of a cloth bag and jammed it on the nail shaft that stuck up at the end of the plank just above the water line. "When you check these traps, Henry, bring apples or carrots to reset the bait—whatever's half rotten and ready to give away."

We walked down about a quarter mile to a deeper section of the creek upstream from the larger boulders that lined the shore. Beavers are more powerful animals than muskrats or rabbits. They swim underwater, so their traps must be heavier and larger. These traps always take longer to set because they require nailing poles and crossbars to the trap so it can be easily retrieved. After setting several traps, Stanley moved back toward the bank and crouched down in order to create a scent mound meant to lure the beaver in the direction of the trap. He made a small pile of mud and sprinkled it with a few drops of beaver lure he'd mixed the previous winter. The creek's dull clamor prevented any conversation. Jim and I stood nearby under a beech tree next to a dense thicket of tangled brush, our eyes fixed on Stanley's preparations.

Kneeling twenty feet directly in front of us, Stanley finished the trap and raised his head to speak. For an instant, his eyes blinked rapidly and his jaw hung loose. His face twisted as it registered alarm and fear. In one swift movement of superior strength he lunged forward hurling Jim and me to the ground and howling violently.

The bear was close enough to smell. My breath caught in my chest as the heavy black figure plunged forward through the brush, grunting and drooling, its thick legs moving quickly toward Stanley who stood firmly in its path. I rose unsteadily to my knees as Stanley waved his arms high above his head and growled in a deep trembling voice. As he stared down the bear, he called loudly to me and Jim, "Back away slowly out of his sight, then run like the devil outta here."

Halting its charge, the bear stood upright on its hind feet sniffing the air. Moaning and popping its jaws, the bear moved closer in Stanley's direction. Its snout shone with moisture, and saliva seeped from its mouth. The bear rushed within a foot of Stanley's face, then withdrew on all fours, its belly hanging low to the ground. Stanley continued his harsh low growl glaring at the back of the bear's broad head as it moved away. I breathed a silent sigh of relief.

In an instant, the bear wheeled about. At full height on its back legs, claws curled in the air, the bear attacked. One large paw slapped at Stanley's chest while the other sliced his back. As Stanley screamed and punched, the bear clamped its jaws around his right shoulder. Massive brown teeth pressed against Stanley's skin where his thin jacket had ripped away. Grunting and drooling, the bear began to shake Stanley like a rag doll.

I stood trembling and confused, feet too heavy to move, my mind numbed by the sudden violence. I could not think what to do, but knew I had to act now to save my brother. The bear's teeth were dangerously close to his face and head.

I checked to see that Jim was safely out of the way, and then picked up the large beech branch at my feet. Terrified, I lurched forward with the branch in both hands, swinging madly; hitting any part of the bear I could reach. With all my strength I lifted the branch above my head and brought it down squarely on the bear's broad snout, striking it over and over again. The bear turned and snarled. I waited for it to come at me. My lips dry, my legs shaking, I stared into the bear's small eyes and braced myself for the second attack. His eyes held mine. The bear veered away toward the creek bed. Panting heavily it rushed past me to the shallow water, clambered up the opposite bank and was gone. I had no notion of how long the attack lasted, but it felt like a lifetime.

Stanley lay perfectly still on the ground, his eyes closed. I counted four puncture wounds on his hands and arms, deep scratches on his neck and face. His shoulder had taken the worst of it. The bite went down to the bone. I gently lifted his head and saw the blood seeping from his back. As I laid my hand on his heart, I prayed to feel it beating.

"Jim," I yelled, "Get the trap pack. Rip that sack cloth. Wet it down with creek water, and bring it here, fast." I fished a large handkerchief from my pants pocket and handed it to Jim as he brought the dripping sack to me. "Wash this out and wet it down real good. Be careful on the rocks." My voice sounded snappish and far away, but Jim obeyed without a word as I carefully washed out the scratches on Stanley's body.

Over the years, my father cautioned us about the bites of wild animals. Most commonly foxes, skunks and raccoons are known to deliver vicious bites, and the risk of infection is considerable. We steer clear of such animals, and they of us. When he was seven, a red fox gave my cousin Woodrow a nasty bite on his hand. I remembered my mother and aunt washing the wound thoroughly, and covering it with salve and a broad bandage.

Jim and I would need a lot of water to wash out the shoulder wound. The skin was badly torn. Quickly, we had to put pressure on to stop the bleeding. I removed Stanley's boots and instructed Jim to fill them with water from the creek. Jim waited while I poured the icy liquid into and around each wound, spending most of it on the gaping shoulder. He hurried back to the creek for more. I folded the jagged skin over the wound and wrapped my wet handkerchief up under Stanley's right arm and around his right shoulder, tying it tightly above his collarbone. I pressed down hard with the heel of my hand. Jim and I worked as best we could, given the darkening sky and our lack of proper experience and tools.

My brother's faint heartbeat and ragged breathing told us he was alive, but he'd lost a lot of blood. The scratches were serious. His skin was cool. I reckoned partly from the creek water and partly from the many shocks his body had endured. I used his own shirt and light jacket to cover much of his upper body and threw my own jacket on top of them as he lay on the ground. Stanley sighed and rolled his head, but in the time since the attack ended, he had neither opened his eyes nor spoken. We surely needed help in moving him, but none was at hand. Our home was a good two miles distant through the woods. The town of Friendsville, while closer, was still a mile away. The sky had grown dark and the air colder. I couldn't risk leaving Jim with Stanley while I went for help, or sending Jim out alone. Luckily, the moon was full.

At first I figured the two of us could carry Stanley along the creek path until we reached the higher ground trail that would lead us to town and Dr. Steele's place. Facing forward, Jim put his hands under Stanley's knees and knelt between them while I held Stanley's chest and head from behind. We could manage if we walked slowly. Carefully, we positioned Stanley's body and prepared to lift him. After a few determined but staggering steps, we knew the weight was too much to bear for more than a short distance. Tears stung our eyes as we pondered our failure. Our frustration was clear.

Jim's body sagged. "I can do it," he sobbed, "I'll try harder. He saved us from that bear. I'm strong enough to save him. He can't die. I won't let him die."

"Take off your jacket, Jim, and lay it flat. We need two or three solid tree limbs. Can you find them? Don't go too far off. Just look around where you stand." As Jim gathered up the sturdy branches, I removed my own jacket from across Stanley's body and took off my shirt. I buttoned up both the jackets and shirt, turned them inside out leaving the sleeves inside, and laid them on the ground one above the other. Jim and I stripped the extra branches and twigs from the limbs so that each one resembled a long straight pole. Working at each end, we passed the poles through the sleeves and pulled them tight across to form a carrying litter. Shaking from the cool air, I rubbed my hands hard over my arms, took a deep shuddering breath, and smiled at our contraption.

Our satisfaction was brief. A look at Stanley told us we had no time to squander on useless celebration. By the light of the moon, we noted a darkening of his skin, a bluish color in his face and neck. And his shoulder was bleeding again, most likely from our feeble attempts at carrying him. Slowly, we rolled him onto his stomach in the direction of the litter and then tipped his body back so he rested on his back on the broad side of both jackets. He gasped softly as we positioned his chilled body in the center of the carrier. Jim and I glanced hopefully at one another, heartened at this weak sign of life. Tightly, we each clutched the forward ends of our poles. We groaned as we heaved the poles upward onto our shoulders. I saw the pole dig sharply into Jim's slim shoulder, but he did not complain. Slowly, we dragged our brother towards town.

Chapter Five

I tried not to feel the cold air against my exposed body or the effort each step cost. Instead, I listened for Stanley's breathing and watched the rise and fall of his chest. The full moon lit our way, and the silence of supreme effort passed between Jim and me. His usually funny face looked drawn and determined, certainly older than its nine years. His hair, like mine, lay wet against his forehead, the result of sweat and worry. I realized that, in the length of an hour, our relationship had changed, and my regard for him had grown. Selfishly, I hoped he felt the same about me.

It was hard to judge how far we'd come. Although I could hear the creek's dull babble, I could no longer see it. For the past few minutes, we'd traveled on a slight incline climbing toward higher ground and the main road into town. We stopped to rest. Rather than drop the poles, we wisely kept them atop our shoulders, knowing we had spent the energy necessary to raise them again. Jim's back was stooped from the weight of the litter and his legs trembled.

"When we get to the road, Jim, you know it's more than a quarter mile into town. I want you to run hard to Dr. Steele's place. I'll stay with Stanley."

"No, Henry, let me stay with him," he pleaded, "I'll watch out for him and keep him warm. Besides, I can't run as fast as you."

My first thought was to bully him into doing what I said. I didn't want him out here in the dark unprotected. No telling how long it would take to rouse Dr. Steele, make clear the situation, and get back.

But, as I said, our relationship had changed.

I smiled tiredly and replied, "I'm glad you recall I beat you last week in that foot race around the barn. It'll take me a little while. We'll find a spot to set him down, out of the woods and off the road. You'll need to keep an eye out for night critters. They'll smell blood and be on him." My voice was hard and serious. I wanted Jim to understand the dangers.

Jim's eyes grew large as he turned his head toward Stanley. I reckoned Jim was rethinking his request. He surprised me when he asked, "Are there any matches in Stanley's pack?"

Once the sun disappears, the road to town is deserted. So we closed in on it before we knew it. We located a flat place and rid it of stones and twigs before setting down the litter. Searching Stanley's pockets we found a box of dry matches and hurriedly built a small fire. Before I left, I checked Stanley's pulse and put my cheek against his mouth so that I could feel his breath. Both acts saddened me, and I took his hands in mine and rubbed them forcefully. He did not stir. As Jim stood close by, I took a final look in his direction and raced off into the night.

The road curves to the west as it enters town. To keep up my speed, I allowed my body to drift toward its center and got a good line as I cut right down Maple Street. I spotted the dark windows of our general store and caught a brief movement on Dr. Steele's porch. When I judged the shadow to be his, I gathered in a huge breath and hollered as loudly as I could, "Help, we need help, please help."

His head and his body turned alertly in my direction as he pushed from his chair and stepped off the porch toward me. Chest heaving, I fell into his shoulder and gasped, "Stanley's hurt real bad. A bear got him down near the creek. Lost a lot of blood. Come quick. You've got to come."

Without hesitation, Dr. Steele directed, "Stay right here, Henry. I'll get my bag and the car. You'll show me where he is."

At some point, I bent my head forward, hands gripping my knees. My chest rattled with exhaustion and momentary relief.

As I climbed into his car, Dr. Steele tossed me several towels and an old wool shirt that smelled like camphor. "Warm yourself, Henry, and tell me all you can about Stanley's condition."

I had begun to recount the events when we spotted the small fire on the left of the roadside. I said a silent prayer when we caught sight of Jim crouched next to Stanley, one hand on Stanley's forehead for comfort (whose I'm not sure), the other holding a long stick for protection.

In one abrupt movement, Dr. Steele braked the car and jumped from it. He headed in a straight line for Stanley as I fetched his bag and light beacon.

"Is he alive?" Jim asked cautiously.

After a few silent moments, came the grim reply. "Barely; that shoulder needs attention. His body's in shock."

The three of us gently lifted Stanley into the car, and laid him carefully across the seat, his shoulder propped between the towels and the upright portion of the seat. I sat on the floor holding his head as we sped back to town in the Ford Coupe. At that point, I felt an urgent need to see my mother and father and tell them of both Stanley's condition and our whereabouts. But I saw no way to accomplish that duty. There was no telephone in our home.

As Dr. Steele drove, Jim and I described the events that took place before, during and after the bear attack, particularly our attempts at first aid and tending to Stanley's wounds. Thinking hard, Dr. Steele asked us to repeat our accounts of the bear's actions and the location of the attack. His eyes narrowed and his lips puckered. While he said nothing for several moments, his mind was hard at work.

"Would you suppose that bear was a female? Maybe a sow protecting her cubs?" questioned Dr. Steele. His voice had a hopeful edge.

"Nope, I expect it was a male," I remarked, "too big for a female. I'd say over 300 pounds and, standing on his back legs, a mite taller than Stanley."

In the heavy silence that followed, I understood the reason for Dr. Steele's questions. Panicked once more, I stammered, "You're thinking that bear was rabid. That's why he attacked. Isn't that so?"

"It's purely possible, Henry, purely possible. Without good cause bears aren't likely to attack humans."

I was deeply aware of the implications of this possibility. I swallowed a miserable sob before it could pass my lips.

"But we were in that bear's territory," I argued from the back seat, "he was hunting for food around those beech trees along the creek. That's all it was. You don't know anything about bears." Suddenly, I felt a confused anger. I was halfway between scared and mad. Jim and I carried our brother to a safe place, where he could get help and get well. Now, he was in danger again. Nothing was certain. Instead of helping us, Rufus Steele was doing his level best to complicate matters. Sitting on the floor of the coupe, my knees against my chin, I laid my forehead against Stanley's side and felt a hot tear slide down my cheek.

Back in 1931, more than a dozen men in Sang Run set out to find a big black bear that mauled and ran off with some livestock in the woods around Ralph Hoye's farm. After Alvin DeWitt shot him, the group tied the 400-pound bear to Wayne DeWitt's right front fender and drove the beast through town. Mr. DeWitt's hound dog sat upright on top of the dead bear and barked the whole time. It was the first bear killed in those parts in over 40 years. Later, when its head was studied, the forest bureau reported the bear was rabid. Luckily, none of the hunters or dogs required rabies treatment.

"Your brother's alive because of what you boys did to save him," declared Dr. Steele as he carefully removed the stained clothing, sack cloth, and handkerchief. "He couldn't have lasted long out there with these injuries. You did a fine job cleaning out these bites and scratches." With our help, the doctor washed the wounds with iodine soap, stitched closed the chest and shoulder gashes, and loosely bandaged them. As we worked to repair Stanley's body, Dr. Steele commended our crude first aid treatments and praised our rough inventions. Heads bowed, neither Jim nor I responded aloud to such compliments, but at their conclusion we turned our lowered heads slightly in the other's direction and smiled. Such was the extent of our celebration.

With blankets and a low fire, Stanley warmed sufficiently so that the blue tint left his skin, replaced by a pinkish flush. Our contentment rose considerably when he fluttered his eyelids and murmured softly, "I thought I told you worthless boys to run." Then, once more, he lapsed into a deep unconsciousness.

Medical tasks completed, Dr. Steele turned to the need to tell my parents of their sons' whereabouts and conditions. He called Ray McConnell who immediately carried the message up the road to our farmhouse. When my father arrived, Stanley was lying quietly, and, according to Dr. Steele, his breathing and heartbeat were regular. The night ended in hushed conversation. Though I listened hard, my father's low voice and my own exhaustion prevented a good understanding of the discussion. I managed to make out "rabies treatment" among the many muffled phrases. I didn't exactly know what "rabies treatment" amounted to or how it came to be available in our town. For the second time that night, I was forced to put my faith in Rufus Steele's ability and judgment. I felt uneasy about it, real uneasy. But Stanley was alive. That's all that counted for now.

Chapter Six

The weeks that followed our family's crisis were spent in and around the farmhouse preparing for the coming winter, coaxing my brother's healing (accompanied in large part through teasing and Jim's practical jokes), and attending to Stanley's schedule of rabies treatments. The latter task fell principally to my mother who, among her other household duties, labored over bandages, herbal salves and plasters. I doubt that Dr. Steele approved of these home remedies, but I noticed no criticism from him. More than once when he turned up to dispense Stanley's daily injection, Dr. Steele listened intently as my mother described her various herbs and the measures she took to keep us well through the winter. Every night before bedtime, she explained, all members of our household are obliged to drink a cup of hot ginger tea, prepared with fresh cream and sugar. As a result, she insisted, no one ever takes sick with colds or flu. In fact, we are a pretty healthy lot.

Stanley's injuries healed quickly, but he was left with limited use of his right shoulder and less than half a middle finger on that hand. The finger was bit off clean at the middle knuckle. In our haste that tense evening, we somehow failed to notice that missing finger piece. Later, Jim and I made efforts to find its remains, but our search turned up no more than a few beaver claws. In any case, Stanley, Jim and I agreed a stubby middle finger was small price to pay for wrestling with a bear.

Winter proves the most difficult of seasons. Even so, I look forward to its hardships and its rewards. When we aren't in school or working at the store, winter preparations take up most of our time. Once the harvesting is done and before the snows arrive, we dig a big dirt pit beside the house, line it with straw and oversized leaves, and fill it with dozens of green apples picked from our back orchard and small potatoes dug from the patch. When the apples and potatoes are laid in, we layer the pit with more straw and leaves and finish it off with a thin covering of moist dirt. Of course, we place markers along the pit's perimeter, so we can find it when the snow falls. Throughout the winter when we desire apples or potatoes, we dig them up a few at a time. They stay fresh and are good to eat all winter.

From the first time I helped my father and older brother complete this chore, I judged it to be one of my favorites. The acts of pitching, catching and juggling across the pit's divide have brought me moments of utter contentment. Between catches, I can snatch a quick bite and feel the warm apple juice run down my chin. More than once, I've been caught with a green apple in my jaw as the next hail of potatoes comes flooding in. I like to inhale the sour freshness of the apples and breathe in the potato's scent. As I close my fist around them, I admire each their small round perfections. I have decided the very nature of the pit and its simple contents appeal to me in a way I cannot explain. Oftentimes, the gap is wide between knowing a thing deep inside and putting it to words.

We use straw to insulate many things against the cold, especially our water pump which is built in a lean-to shelter against the east side of the house. The big pump handle works fine most winter mornings—although the priming takes some force. My mother insists on maintaining a full tank of hot water at all times. The water tank, attached to the wood stove, is readily accessible for our daily bathing, my father's morning shave, and Monday's laundering. Each morning when we bring in the water buckets, my mother immediately fills the tank to the brim. Surprisingly, it takes but a few minutes for the stove's warmth to change the cold water to hot.

From the time I was a small boy, my father's morning shave held my full attention, especially in the winter time. I can picture the order of things before it happens. With her left hand, my mother removes the white enamel pan from the nail where it hangs above the kitchen cupboard. We replaced that nail not too long ago. In the same movement, she sets the pan on the ledge below the mirror that's suspended above the cupboard. She tips the kettle forward so that a clear stream of hot water stops just before it fills the pan. My father appears and places his rough hands into the steaming pan, rubbing them together as the steam rises from it. He places one hot hand on each cheek. He does this several times, finally rubbing his hands together to rid them of any excess water. After sharpening his razor five times on the strop that's attached to the side of the cupboard, he lathers his hands with soap and water and lays the lather on both sides of his face, his chin and, lastly, his upper lip. He peers into the mirror and uses his left hand to pull his face tight. In his right hand he holds the sharpened razor. With perfect precision, he draws it slowly across his left cheek, and then dips it into the basin, turning it over so that each side is cleaned and ready for the next stroke. With the same movement, he clears his right cheek, his chin, and his upper lip of a day's worth of whiskers. He uses a warm towel to remove the last bits of soap from the tips of his ears and the base of his chin. When the thickening fuzz on my own jaw requires me to perform this duty,

I doubt that I'll be able to begin each new day with the same self assured smoothness and sure hand as my father, but I aspire to do so.

If the temperature dips below freezing and remains there for a good long time, it's likely to be a miserable morning. The pump freezes up, and we have to tote water in from the spring. The spring house lies a good distance from the back door. In the dark quiet morning, I pass the time by listening to the trickling water and the clang of the bucket as it fills. It is indeed the most delicious water. Still, the walk back up the home path with a full bucket of sloshing icy water has always been my most detested chore.

On the other hand, crackling cold mornings when the snow stands deep on the ground and an icy crust crunches underfoot hold their own appeal. Such mornings, I privately compete to be the first footprint on the snow's pure surface, the first hand on the jagged icicle, the first to watch my breath turn to a steamy puff. There is a satisfaction in being first.

In a bitter cold, the cows' water buckets and feed bins have to be cleared of the ice layers that form during the night. Now and then, those cows bless me with a thankful expression before plunging their noses into their morning oats. Inside our kitchen, I offer my mother the same grateful tribute as she places bowls of hot oatmeal and loaves of hot bread under our noses.

I cup my frozen hands under and around the oatmeal bowl to coax warmness back to my fingers.

In a heavy snow, we're lucky to get to school or town or church services. If the snow is not too deep, we can ride our sleds straight down the road from our house to Buffalo Bridge and pull them the last half mile to school. Early each winter, my father repairs our old sleds. If the beds or runners are splintered or broken, he builds a new one, moving in time to the pace of his favorite hymn. I reckon all our sleds' runners hum a version of *Amazing Grace* as they skim the crust of the snow. When a new sled is finished, we are impatient for the chance to test it out, soaring and whooping down the hillside. Over the hill above our house snow drifts can reach 10 to 15 feet high, especially in high winds. A few good sled runs pack the snow down pretty good.

On the severest weather days my father is unable to work, so he spends his time digging out a path to the barn, the smoke house, and the spring. Later in the day, armed with a basket of fresh eggs and instructions from my mother, my father hikes the half mile to Nolan Kendall's small store to buy groceries that will last until we can reach our own store in town. Unlike our larger general store, Kendall's sells essentials such as bread, cheese, baloney, butter, ammunition, gasoline, my mother's eggs, and candy. Much to our disappointment, my mother fiercely refuses to allow my father to buy so much as one piece of sweet candy at Kendall's. If you've spent any time at all around Nolan Kendall, you know he sneezes a lot and blows his nose thereafter. Unfortunately, Nolan does not possess a handkerchief and instead blows into his hand on these occasions. That same hand is used to gather fistfuls of candy from the jar he keeps below his payment counter. Thus, no Kendall sweets have ever entered our home or passed our lips. We gather, however, our share of homemade sweet candy. Using the syrup we tap from the dozen black sugar maples in our front yard, my mother makes us maple syrup candy patties. Indeed, they are delicious!

For the past 100 years, the average season's snowfall in Garrett County hangs around 80 inches. On heavy snow days, it's impossible to clear out a path for an automobile. The snows heap themselves heavily against the outbuildings and along the roads so they are impassable. A neighbor might manage to dig out a lighter vehicle and ride a short distance on the top crust of snow. The car finally sinks, however, and all available men and boys in the area are rounded up to lift the car out and set it down on solid ground. Our particular road inclines sharply over a short bumpy rise located about a tenth of a mile before our driveway turns off up to the house. Even on dry winter days, we've had to abandon our car or wagon, unable to get a firm grip over the icy bulge. One Christmas morning, our kinfolk had cause to leave their cars behind and trudge uphill the remaining 200 yards to our front door. My father and Stanley stood astride the slippery knob and helped each person find a way over the frozen patches. They struggled several times, and Stanley nearly lost his balance before Grandma Fearer finally made it up the hill. She'd lost her footing twice, rolled around a good bit, and lost a few holiday presents in the effort. We laughed wildly, covering our mouths with both hands, as Stanley later reported this episode. Of course, we lowered our heads and scattered quickly when my mother, on her way to the pantry to store her annual gift of medicinal whiskey, inquired about our noisy behavior.

That icy little hill was sufficient reason for our mailman, Albert Krug, to keep a tended horse in a small barn near Blooming Rose junction. This arrangement allowed him to drive his car from town, park at the bottom of the hill, transfer our local letters and packages to the horse's saddle bags, and make his daily deliveries up the mountain—even in a driving snowstorm. As near as I can remember, Albert Krug never missed a delivery—until, of course, the first week in February 1939.

Chapter Seven

The new year's first snow started to fall before dawn on Monday, January 30 and kept falling until the following Sunday. The snow was deep in every direction. The path we cleared to the barn each morning was closed by the end of the day, so we began again at first light the next day, barely able to see the edge of our shovels. The animals had to be fed and watered, and the cows needed milking. They piled together at one end of the barn for what warmth they could make. As close as they stood, it was a wonder they did not suffocate one another.

Most of that week was bitter cold. The hard frost on the ground was covered with new snow, making each step icy and treacherous. Even for Garrett County, it was unusual weather. It was rare to see anyone on the roads as many were drifted shut with packed snow and ice. Families remained at home, missing school and church services. Workers from the County Roads Department battled a sixteen-foot snowdrift that completely blocked the road halfway between Friendsville and McHenry. It took the road crew seven hours to cut a path by hand through the frozen drift. People stood by their cars along the road watching and waiting. Even the snow fences along the roadside could not contain the massive drifts that buried the crossbars on the telephone poles. Snow kept falling.

On Thursday as we finished the last of our usual morning business, Uncle Frank came riding up the yard on his chestnut mare. The sky's color was a dull maroon. Through the fresh falling snowflakes, Uncle Frank looked a pinkish gray as he climbed down from his horse.

"Worst snowstorm I've seen. Got drifts prit near 12 feet against my porch. Gauge says 20 inches fell in the last two days. Thermometer reads 10 degrees and below. I've an idea worse weather's coming. Animals are near freezing. Can't hardly keep 'em alive in this cold. Three young calves run off last night. I fear they're caught in a snowdrift and likely to starve." He stomped his boots hard and brushed his hat free of snow before he entered the kitchen. Uncle Frank owned dozens of cows, and his dairy provided milk, cream, cheese, and butter for much of Garrett County. Losing a portion of his herd, especially the fragile calves, would prove costly.

My father replied seriously, 'If that's true, Frank, you won't find them until the snow melts. They'll be hard to track with all this new snow. Looks like a blizzard, maybe an ice storm, blowing in across the mountains."

"Sure could use your help, Andrew. Woodrow and Glenn set out to the lower field to search down into the coves. Figured those calves would move downhill. But there's more pasture to cover. Snow stands knee-deep in places. Out in these temperatures, neither calves nor boys last long."

There wasn't much time for thinking about my uncle's request. "Get your things, Henry. Strap a shovel to each horse, and remember to attach the sleigh bells onto the saddles. We'll need them in this weather. Do you have enough rope for those calves, Frank?" Only after he'd reached for his jacket and gloves did my father chance to look at my mother standing near the stove. "Warm your hands before you venture out," she advised.

Riding side by side up the road ahead of me, my father and his brother looked to be the same person. Their height, weight, the cock of their heads, placement of their hats, and position in the saddle were identical. In truth, there are many differences between them, not least of which involves their sons. In due time, that piece of history will reveal itself as one of the more remarkable family stories. This particular morning, however, I hurried to keep up with the larger and swifter animals. Nellie, our old plow horse, moved slowly through the cold morning, her old bones craving the comfort and shelter of the barn. At the south gate, we turned off the road and headed cautiously into the larger pasture. The gathering snow at its base made it near impossible to push open the gate. By the time I rehung the latch and climbed back on my horse, I could not see my father's nor my uncle's figures ahead of me. Nor could I see much further than my own outstretched glove. A bleak, foggy haze had settled on the pasture making it difficult to detect even the closest object. Tightly, I held Nellie's reins in one hand and placed the other on her warm shoulder until my eyes adjusted in the dim light, fearful that I sat lost in a blurry white space. I likened the image before me to the inside of a goose feather pillow—swirling white snow against a solid white background. Luckily, I could hear the bells on the forward horses, and followed that sound for a few hundred yards, relieved finally to recognize two familiar figures. As the snows deepened around the horses' hooves we reckoned it unlikely we'd find any tracks for those calves. I pulled the ear flaps of my wool cap down around my jaw, tied it tightly, tucked the laces inside my neckerchief, and gave Nellie's neck a good rub, immediately glad for her company.

Although we had walked or ridden this pasture hundreds of times, it looked like a foreign place. Snow piles, driven by the wind, were heaped against one another, each mound higher than the one that abutted it. Large tree limbs hung low to the ground, heavy with snow and ice, ready to break. We came upon them suddenly in the pale light. For almost an hour, we rode with only the sound of sleigh bells and the horses' breathing marking our way. Occasionally, one of the horses would harrumph loudly and throw his head from side to side to clear his ears and nose of snow and ice crystals.

At once, we heard a distant sound. In the gray coldness, a calf bayed. Amidst the white expanse, we and the horses stood quietly, all ears alert and searching. Satisfied with our direction, we moved closer to the sound. My father spotted faint footprints leading down a narrow path above the creek bed. As the fog lifted, we made out the top of the calf's head. He stood in the frozen stream, stuck among the rocks not able to free himself to climb up the bank. Two younger calves huddled together nearby, powerless to help their stranded friend yet unwilling to leave him behind. I roped them in and tied them one to the other to Nellie's saddle horn. Neither calf protested. From the looks of them, they had stood in that same place for some time. Thick snow clung to their bodies, their eyes nearly frozen shut, their ears straight and brittle. As I wiped their broad faces with my neckerchief, I heard the soft tinkling of their eyelashes.

Meanwhile, Uncle Frank was figuring a way to get the last calf up the creek bank without freezing his own feet in the effort. But it was clear the calf's hooves were wedged in amongst the rocks, and I reckoned they were frozen as well. As I got closer, I spotted a thick red stripe behind the calf's left ear.

"This animal's hurt," my father observed. "Must have got caught up on a barbed wire. Looks like he's lost some blood, judging by that wide gash. It won't do to put a rope around his neck."

"We can't leave him out here. Need to get him back to the barn so I can care for that wound," said my uncle.

Just as my mother cares for the physical state of the human members of our family, likewise my father and his brother are skilled animal healers. Using herbal and animal fat mixtures, they make ointments and poultices for curing the cows and horses of assorted ailments. The poultices work especially well in treating puncture and abscess wounds, where a build-up of infection needs to be drawn out. Many of our farm animals owe their healthy condition to my uncle's concoctions of skunk oil and herbs.

As we stood conversing on ways to free the calf and return the three strays to the shelter of Uncle Frank's barn, I felt a presence at my back. I turned abruptly to see a gray figure emerge from the white pasture, approaching on foot. Hands in his coat pockets and shoulders hunched against the wind, the man carried a backpack and moved awkwardly atop a pair of oversized snowshoes. Once again, I admired that handsome gray hat he wore, now covered in a layer of snow.

"Glad to see you boys." His voice propelled itself against the wind and falling snow. "I followed the sound of your horse bells and trusted I'd come upon you sooner or later. I'm glad it was sooner."

My father reached an arm toward him and asked, "What brings you out this way, Dr. Steele? This weather's not fit for travel, especially on foot."

Rufus Steele considered his reply for a moment and remarked, "Got some patients on this mountain and couldn't get my car past your bump in the road. I found these old snowshoes and decided to take a walk. On the last hill, I met your boys, Frank, who told me where you might be. Wondered if I could lend a hand, but it looks as if you've found your missing calves."

"We found them all right, but one's clean stuck in that creek yonder. Don't reckon how I can get him unstuck without stepping out on that ice," said Uncle Frank.

Even at its highest point in the spring of the year, the stream does not measure more than three to four feet in depth. Its surface appeared to be solid, but it was hard to say whether the ice was thick enough to hold both a man's weight and the calf's. We could hear the water moving beneath the surface of ice. My father tied a large knot at the end of a rope and hurled it several times at the calf's hindquarters, trying to budge him from his spot. Each time the knot hit the calf we whooped and hollered in an effort to scare him into motion. But the calf stood fixed in place, wailing mournfully into the harsh bitter air. Something had to be done quickly. We'd all been out too long in the cold.

Uncle Frank stepped carefully down the embankment onto the frozen stream. For a moment he stood upright on its surface and deliberately bounced once, applying his full weight to the ice floor. It seemed solid enough. Cautiously, he strode the last few steps that separated him and the calf. He knelt beside the scared animal and lifted its front hooves out of the stones and ice fragments. Uncle Frank examined the delicate underside of both hooves and picked out a few sharp pebbles. He tied one end of a sturdy rope around the calf's chest just behind his shaky front legs, and then bent down to loosen the calf's back hooves. My father caught the other end of the rope which he wound around his horse's saddle horn and directed the horse to slowly back away from the stream. The soft jingle of bells marked a steady pace as the horse leaned and pulled backwards until the slack rope stretched tight. Pushing forward against the calf's hindquarters, Uncle Frank gave him a hard shove from behind. Immediately, I heard a sharp crack and watched transfixed as the ice broke apart under Uncle Frank's feet. The black water bubbled swiftly up his pants legs. With a loud gasp (and a swear word the preacher would not approve), Uncle Frank sank waist deep into the creek. He struggled to keep his footing while he searched for the surest way up the embankment, but large ice chunks blocked his path. Within a few seconds the water's swiftness lifted his body and carried him downstream. As we watched, he hung suspended on a group of rocks, his heavy wet clothing and rushing ice fragments pulling him backward into the water so he was unable to right himself.

Quickly shrugging his pack to the ground and releasing his snowshoes, Rufus Steele grabbed a rope from the horse's saddle and ran along the bank opposite to where Uncle Frank lay on his back in the stream. Dr. Steele tied the rope securely around his own waist and threw the loose end in my direction. Still busy with the calf and his horse, my father hollered to me to grab the rope and stretch it tight when needed. As Dr. Steele jumped from boulder to boulder across the stream, I fumbled to provide enough rope for his positions. When he reached Uncle Frank, Dr. Steele grabbed the back of my uncle's coat collar and jerked hard to force Uncle Frank's head and shoulders upright out of the water. With two strong hands working against the black water, Dr. Steele held on and dragged Uncle Frank's body onto the rocks to a high boulder in midstream. Uncle Frank let out a feeble groan as he lay perched across the rock.

"Looks like your leg's broken, Frank. Got to get you out of your wet clothes before your body temperature drops too low. I'm going to pass this rope around your chest, and position you upright. Then Henry is going to pull you forward while I push you from behind up that embankment. Give me a little more rope, Henry, so I can untie myself. I'll yell when we're ready for you to yank it nice and easy. First, we've got to find a firm spot on these icy rocks. Then we'll get as close as we can to the bank."

By that time, my father had tied up the injured calf and stood alongside me. We waited for the doctor's signal as we anxiously watched him and my uncle slipping sideways off the edges of the frozen rocks. The waters rose around their feet as the ice continued to be washed downstream. I gripped the rope as Dr. Steele fell to his knees and nearly lost his footing. With no safety line, his position was as dangerous as my uncle's. Steadying himself, Dr. Steele passed the rope under Uncle Frank's arms several times so that it covered a good portion of his ribs. Then the doctor tied a knot in the center of Uncle Frank's chest. His fractured left leg made it impossible for my uncle to balance himself or move under his own power. His big frame shuddered with cold as he leaned heavily against Dr. Steele who bore both their weights. Dragging one painful leg behind, Uncle Frank's right arm rested atop the doctor's broad shoulders. Dr. Steele's left arm enveloped Uncle Frank's back, guiding and lifting him toward the embankment. Taking carefully measured steps, Dr. Steele inched them forward. Several times, I feared they would slide on the ice and pitch backward into the dark waters. In these conditions, I doubted that my father and I could rescue them both, and suddenly I was overcome with uncertainty and dread.

My desperation passed, however, as they crept closer to a low spot on the stream's bank. I clutched the rope, ready for the right moment to pull my uncle to safety.

"Now, Henry!" came the booming voice. "Tighten up that rope and move on back with it. Don't let him slip into the water."

When Dr. Steele released his hold, I was not prepared for my uncle's full weight, and I stumbled forward letting the rope go slack for an instant. Thankfully, my father stood behind me and, with great force, yanked me and the rope backward. I had forgotten how strong his many years of lumbering and farming had made him. We pulled steadily, backtracking in the deep snow, marching together, one foot with another, straining against the heaviness of Uncle Frank's wet clothes and resistant leg. Finally, Uncle Frank's form rose stiffly from the bank and fell forward onto the snow. We rushed to untie the rope and strip the clothes from his body.

Over the years, we'd had our share of frostbite scares when we remained outside too long in the winter cold. Luckily, there'd been no permanent damage to our fingers or toes. While my brothers and I were neither concerned nor careful about exposing our various body parts to the cold, my mother insisted that our noses and ears be covered. Every winter she knitted us fresh toboggan hats, mittens, and nose warmers. In truth, we were not overly fond of the nose warmers. They quickly disappeared into a jacket pocket the moment she lost sight of us.

But Uncle Frank's condition was worse than a frostbite scare. As he lay on the ground before us, his muscles twitched, and his body shook. He stuttered rather than spoke. A bone in his lower left leg protruded slightly from the skin. While my father stayed close beside him, I ran to loosen the saddle from his horse—enough to slide the blanket from beneath it. The animal's warmth—from his back to his belly—clung to the underside of the wool blanket. My father placed it carefully under his brother and motioned for me to retrieve the other blankets. I didn't say anything, just nodded a time or two and ran off to harvest Nellie's natural heat. With the second blanket we covered the entire length of Uncle Frank's body, wrapping it around his shoulders, neck and head. The third blanket we draped across his chest, an added layer to warm his heart. We tucked his arms and hands, legs and feet under the layers of wool. His sudden immersion in the cold water and his wet clothing had cooled his body to a dangerously low temperature. Warming it again was vital. We did not know the extent of damage already caused by the intense cold.

Rufus Steele struggled up the embankment. As he walked toward us, I saw the quick flashes of a small hunting knife he applied to strip the smaller twigs from two dead tree branches he turned in his hands. Satisfied with their length and smoothness, the doctor knelt on my uncle's left side and gently laid back one edge of the blanket. With one hand on the base of Uncle Frank's knee, Dr. Steele pressed down hard. His other hand, positioned under Uncle Frank's ankle, jerked up abruptly, and the white bone disappeared into the skin's protective shelter. I saw Uncle Frank grimace and huddle deeper into the blankets. Using a rope, the doctor bound the two branches and the leg into one inseparable piece. As I inspected the rough splint, I felt my muscles tighten and my ears growing numb. The cold air did not relent.

Throughout this painful procedure, my father continued to encourage blood to flow by rubbing Uncle Frank's neck and shoulders. After a short while, Frank determinedly tossed off his brother's hands, raised himself up on one arm, leaned his head forward, and stared at Rufus Steele.

"You boys liken to kill me," my uncle growled, "and I smell like that old plow horse of yourn, Andrew. At least fetch me some of that thermos coffee so I can stop these goll-darn shivers. Agnes'll be going on about these wet clothes. And best not mention my recent cursing of the Lord where she's likely to hear. Doc, how do I suppose to get on my horse with this tree on my leg?"

Amidst the silent snowflakes, Dr. Steele arose from his knees, removed his hat, brushed the snow from its brim, and, with a wink in my direction, replaced it at a sloppy angle.

"Why, Frank, you'll just have to walk home. 'Cause I'm riding that pretty chestnut mare of yours."

Relieved and exhausted, the four of us chuckled and hooted until we cried, and the tears froze hard on our cheeks. We bundled up Uncle Frank and fussed over him until he felt like hot bread from my mother's oven. We sat him up so that he and his splinted leg faced sideways like a great protuberance off the back of one of those wandering calves, then made our way slowly up the hill and out the pasture gate. I breathed a long breath, watched as the wind rattled the trees, and listened to the light jingle of sleigh bells.

I reckon we all made up our minds that day about Rufus Steele.

Chapter Eight

In late April, early morning frosts led us to believe that spring weather was near. But I've learned never to count on the steadiness of Garrett County's temperatures. Falling new snow whitened the high school's May Pole rite. We ended the program with a snowball fight instead of the usual flower procession. As a result, the parlor furnace worked overtime during both winter and spring seasons. At least three times, we revisited our small mining shaft to dig out a load of coal to replenish the stockpile under the house. On each occasion, we returned home with blackened hands and faces—chilled as much by the darkness as by the damp cold of the open shaft.

"That coal vein is just about dry," muttered my father. "We'd best find another before next fall. I'm not inclined to move further into that shaft without proper equipment. Could be Woodrow and Glenn can lend a hand now that Frank's leg is healed. I hate to give up on that tunnel since it's so close to the house, but we can't take a chance on it giving out in mid-winter."

There's plenty of coal in the ground around our farm, particularly in Preston County, West Virginia which touches our property to the west. A small mining community exists up the river. Larger mining companies are located north in Pennsylvania. The B & O Railroad hauls coal cars through the Friendsville station every day of the week. I don't know where they're going to, but they come from coal mines to the west and north of us. Several of my cousins work in the local mines. I think highly of the skill required in their daily labor, and, according to talk in the general store, the pay allows a man to purchase a few extra of life's bits and pieces. But, for one reason or another, I've never given much thought to picking coal. In truth, I'm not keen on dying in the dark.

Along the notions of living and dying, Jim spotted a big white tent on Route 42. It sprang up one morning in a field just north of Friendsville Road. A large-lettered green sign announced the arrival of a couple of revivalist preachers. The first service of their three-day meeting commenced the following night—Friday, May 5 at 7:00, with two more sermons on Saturday and three on Sunday.

"What's a revival, Henry?" questioned Jim.

"Got a lot to do with religion and the Lord," I answered, trying to sound smarter than I was about the subject. "Preachers travel around praying real loud, trying to save people from sin."

"What's the use of traveling preachers? Why don't people just read the Bible, or go to church like we do?" persisted Jim.

He was getting into territory I knew little about. "They're just trying to be useful," I offered. Before I could add another bit of ignorance to our conversation, one of the preachers appeared outside the tent, thumping a ragged Bible, urging all who passed to listen to the Good Book and the power of the Holy Spirit.

"We have all sinned. Be washed white, and be saved by the glory of God," he bellowed. "Turn away from sin. Repent or perish. Assure yourselves of God's glory for all eternity."

Obviously, Jim and I had never been to a revival meeting and were attracted to what that traveling preacher might have to say, especially about the Holy Spirit. The minute we walked through our door, Jim started in pestering my mother about going to the revival meeting. After supper, he followed her around the kitchen as she swept the day's dirt, crumbs, and ashes out the back door. He even interrupted the evening radio program. Finally, she relented—as much so she could hear the news as any other reason.

"Those preachers go on too severe about the devil's possession," she remarked, "instead of obedience to the Golden Rule. You and Henry go hear for yourselves, but don't come home babbling about the chains of Satan."

Jim's excitement grew all day Friday. Through supper he fidgeted and fussed and ate nothing but a few potatoes and biscuits. At last the table was cleared. Long about twilight, we grabbed our jackets and headed down the road to the service. I was eager to hear about eternity—since it has always seemed a strange idea to me. We joined the crowds hovering near the tent opening and moved inside to examine the straight rows of chairs facing the dark pulpit. Kerosene lanterns hung outside, casting gray shadows against the yellowed tent. I felt an odd brush of air warm my cheek. I turned to its source, but saw nothing to have caused it. Like my mother instructed, we walked about halfway in and sat in two wooden chairs along the center aisle, Jim on the outside for a better view of the stage. We listened to the steady beat of the gospel music as we waited in the hazy light for the meeting to begin. The tent was packed, the aisles full. Around us, dozens of people swayed back and forth; tapping their feet, humming *Shall We Gather at the River?* I spied Aunt Agnes and Woodrow in the back row bobbing their heads and slapping their knees in rhythm. Three of my school buddies stood together along the side aisles, handy to the exit. We nodded and exchanged toothless grins, hopeful for a full report before math class on Monday morning.

The first preacher, big as a bear with thick black hair, appeared suddenly upon the stage, a Bible under his arm and an iron chain wound around his wrist. As the music faded away he shook his long finger at the crowded room.

"What sayeth the Good Book? What shall I do to be saved? How shall I throw off the chains that pull me down, down into the house of Satan?" He roared as I imagined a lion roared at his jungle enemies. The loosened chain set off flying over the pulpit and landed loudly on center stage. Jolted by the unexpected sound, the assembly sat stiff in its chairs, staring spellbound at the chain, chanting after him the preacher's words.

"Jesus is the answer. Jesus is the answer. Jesus is the answer."

Everyone murmured *Amens* and *Praise the Lords*. With a heavy step a second preacher entered through the rear of the tent. He wore an old fashioned long-tailed coat which, caught in the lantern light, cast a looming shadow. He and his big hands stopped beside Jim's chair. With an arm of considerable length, he seized Jim's now tiny shoulder. "With the word of the Lord, my son, you will be healed," he whispered in a voice that all could hear. Jim folded up, his chin against his knees, as the big man moved toward the pulpit and began to tell a familiar story.

The preacher's voice rang loud inside the tent, "One night, a sinner found himself slipping down the side of a mountain. At last, he caught a branch which stopped his fall. Through the dark night, he clung to that branch. Near dawn, alas, his fingers finally loosed their hold and, as he bade farewell to this life, he let himself fall."

The preacher lowered his voice to the silent crowd. "Brothers and sisters, that sinner fell just six inches to the ground, just six inches. That sinner should have given up the struggle earlier on that dark night."

The tent poles shook as the preacher's words rose upwards to a fiery pitch. Forcefully and unexpectedly, he slammed a chair across the stage as he hollered, "Give up your struggle tonight, sinners. Trust in the Lord. Pray with us. Release the devil's chains." The big preacher clenched his fists and groaned as he sunk to his knees and then sprang up again, a wild look in his eyes.

Jim and I sat very still, scared witless as boys and girls melted from their chairs to the dirt floor; men collapsed around one another; women were carried from the tent fainting and speechless. We gasped and grabbed each other's knees when people rushed the stage to sink upon the "anxious bench"—and make a full confession of their life's sins. The joints on that bench liked to break apart from all the weight upon it and all the rocking and wriggling those sinners did.

The crowd echoed the preacher's words as the collection plates were passed along the aisles and deep into each row.

"Give to God. Give to God. Give to God."

When the metal offering tray arrived, Jim reached into his pocket, squeezed out a shiny nickel, and placed it, precisely and evenly, in the center of the plate, mumbling "Amen." I reckoned he was buying forgiveness for, among other sins, the time he let a lizard loose in Sunday school class. The preacher's wife had grabbed him by the fattest part of his ear and led him to the front of the class. He got a good licking for it. I figured that was punishment enough—no need to waste a nickel on it. 'Course, he could have been thinking about some other sins I had not witnessed firsthand.

Before long, I began to count up my own sins, leastwise the ones the devil might take hold of, and how much they might cost. There was the time I sneaked some smokes in Clyde Glover's hay loft, the few occasions I lied to my teachers about finishing all my homework, and the day I went sledding instead of delivering my mother's eggs straight away to Kendall's store. To my mind, my worst act thus far in life involved two friends, a bunch of green apples in Hayward Clark's orchard, and a big black snake.

It happened one afternoon two summers ago on our way home from fishing below Buffalo Bridge. My friends and I caught three medium-sized yellow perch and a few small suckers. As my father reminded us, successful hunters and fishermen always shared their food, so we meant to carry our catch home for a family fish-fry supper. Since we'd eaten no lunch save a few blackberries from a bush that hung over the shoreline, we were mighty hungry. Our stomachs growled under our light shirts as we marched up the dusty road past the rail fence marking Clark's apple orchard. Mr. Clark made a living selling apples throughout western Maryland, and his orchard enjoyed a good reputation. Plump green apples hung low on the branches, ripe and just ready for picking. With no hesitation, we leaned our poles and worm cans (I couldn't abide keeping them in my pockets) against the fence, climbed through the rail slats, and hungrily charged the nearest trees, pocketing the lowest and best fruit until our pants and arms could hold no more. Even so, we continued tearing apples from their limbs, throwing them into the air, laughing at one another. I can not say why we took more than the few apples needed to soothe our own hunger. A greedy, dizzy rush took hold of us that warm afternoon. Were it not for an angry black snake, we might have destroyed all the apples in that orchard patch. We raced around the trees, searching for the biggest apples to fling sidearm into the ditch across the road, competing for the longest throw. As I grabbed a high branch to pull myself up onto a tree limb, I felt a quick cool movement beneath my hand and jerked it back. The thick dark snake hissed, opening his pink mouth six inches from my own. His tongue leapt out and touched my chin as terror squeezed the breath from my lungs. Like a shot, I turned and vaulted the rail fence in one blind streak. I didn't stop running until sundown. I look back on that afternoon with fright and a kind of shame that will remain with me a long while. Neither a nickel nor endless nights with the devil could begin to repay Hayward Clark for the damage we did to his apple crop that day.

When the preachers' shouting and the assembly's confessions were over, Jim and I shuffled shocked and saucer-eyed out of the shadowy tent, no closer to being righteous true believers than when we'd arrived a few hours earlier, but knowing we'd had our fill of angry revivalist preachers for a good while.

As we reached the exit, I observed Aunt Agnes and Woodrow huddled outside with Rufus Steele. For once, Dr. Steele was without his gray wool hat. I'd forgotten that his hair was light in color. I'd also forgotten to list that old situation with Woodrow amongst my sins.

Chapter Nine

"Steee-rike three; you're out!" ordered the umpire as he extended his arm and pointed at the far bench, ending the first game of the 1939 baseball season with a big 12–0 victory for Friendsville's town team. The Addison Nine hadn't scored a run in our lopsided win, and I was pretty proud of my first shutout of the season.

I can't remember the first time I threw a baseball. But from that day on, I was hooked on the game. Baseball's always been my favorite sport. Playing baseball can make my heart fly high as the sky or drop into my shoes. I'll play any position, but I consider myself a pretty fair pitcher. My second choice is playing center field, racing after fly balls, covering ground like a thoroughbred horse, stretching and diving for a sinking line drive.

When the snows finally melted from Keyser's Ridge and the creeks ran high, we eagerly started our summer baseball league. Early June evenings, before dark, the whole team showed up with rakes, shovels and brooms to restore the Friendsville field. Not far from my father's store, I could work off most of my afternoon shift and make it to the field by 5:00 each day. By that time, all the boys had finished their chores and arrived with what tools they could manage to carry. Before we could measure the base paths, build up the pitcher's mound, and mark home plate, we removed rocks and limbs and leveled out the grass that survived the winter frosts. Each boy took a different edge of the field, and we gradually worked our way toward the center, piling stones and branches together and then dropping them down the steep hill that marked the end of right field. Over the years, as they've run down a high fly ball, we've lost sight of a few right fielders over that embankment. Seconds later, we'll hear a holler. They'll appear with their hat cockeyed and the ball in an outstretched hand, claiming to have caught it while falling over the hill.

The rest of the baseball field stretches out flat from home plate. A stand of loblolly pines used to signal the boundary line for center and left field until Stanley and his friends built a rail fence just in front of it. What with bumping into tree trunks and rolling down hills, we ran short on outfielders for awhile until that fence went up. Now the crows like to sit on its top rail catching the sun and watching the game.

In no time at all, we took inventory of our equipment—such as it was: three bats, two well-used balls, and a catcher's mitt. Each new season, we had to make ourselves a few new balls. Friendsville's knitters and quilters, including Martha Murphy, saved us their leftover knitting yarn and quilting threads to make the extra balls we needed for our practice sessions. In groups of two and three, our team members took turns coiling the threads tight to form a hard center core for each ball. We carried those little coils everywhere, kept them in our pockets, fingered them during classroom lessons, worked on them over lunch sandwiches in the schoolyard before school let out for the summer, and passed them off to fresh hands when our own tired. When the center of the ball was nice and tight, we stretched and wound the softer yarns around the core until it felt hard enough and sat just right in our palms. Finally, we covered the firm ball with thick black tape, smoothing the edges into a fine perfect sphere. The boy who possessed a fresh roll of black tape was the most valuable player on the team. We couldn't make it through any part of the baseball season without black tape. In addition to finishing our balls, that tape held together sundry parts of our three bats and the lacing on the backside of our catcher's mitt. We always kept an eye out for used equipment and picked up and worked to repair what the other local teams threw away or left behind. While we were not the best-equipped team on the western conference fields, for the past two years we'd proved to be the best, beating every team in southwest Pennsylvania and western Maryland within 40 miles.

Since we fielded only nine players on our team, it was important that everyone showed up for every game. On certain days when Albert Hoye's chores weren't done and his mother would forbid him to leave the house until they were, we were forced to play without a shortstop. Albert fancied himself as a young Arky Vaughan, shortstop for the Pirates, because Albert batted lefthanded and threw right-handed—just like Arky. I felt absolutely sure, however, that one of the finest hitting shortstops in professional baseball (Arky batted .322 last season) never recruited his sister to shovel out the barn or had his mother restrict him from the infield. That said, Albert was a pretty good shortstop, and we struggled to cover the hole between second and third during his frequent punishments. Were it not for our third baseman's headfirst catches and flying grabs, we would have suffered defeat in a few big games. For one game, we substituted our right fielder, Ivan Early, at shortstop leaving the center fielder to cover both center and right fields. We rethought that strategy, however, when Ivan made three straight errors in the second inning. Every game thereafter, Ivan played right field.

I modeled my pitching style after Mace Brown, the Pirates right-handed workhorse relief pitcher who won 15 games in 1938, led the National League with

51 games pitched, and earned the MVP award in the 1938 All-Star game after pitching three innings. Mace had two pitches I liked, an overhand curveball and a breaking pitch. Using a nub of chalk, I drew a shaky circle the size of a strike zone on an old tree in our yard and practiced both pitches over and over until they came natural to me. I used them whenever we needed to put away a game. When it got too dark to see the ball, I'd snap off several of those specialty pitches. Batters had to swing on what they heard coming at 'em. That curveball always did the trick.

As I mentioned, our equipment inventory was running mighty low, and we had no way to buy anything new. Every once in a while in seasons past, Stanley's lumber hauls took him south to Oakland or north to Uniontown where, if he'd earned any overtime pay, he made a special stop to buy us a new baseball. Last May, he brought the team a long strip of white ash he picked up in Pennsylvania, enough to make two new bats. However, in the past six months since his run-in with the bear, Stanley had struggled to relearn the routine acts of everyday life. By the start of baseball season he'd more than recovered and was driving a truck once more. But thus far, he'd been unable to replenish either balls or bats for the team.

It was a surprise, then, when Rufus Steele arrived at our practice diamond one afternoon carrying a bulky blue bag across his broad shoulders. Discussing game strategy and vehicle arrangements for tomorrow's game in Swanton, we hardly noticed him or the saggy-eyed, long-eared hound dog that followed close on his heel. All at once, we heard the distinctive clatter of wooden bats falling as Dr. Steele dropped the dusty-looking canvas bag behind home plate and walked our way. The dog assumed a guard-like pose at the far end of the bag.

On that clear and cloudless afternoon, we sat in silence on the visitors' bench munching peanut butter sandwiches and considered the new arrivals.

"Hear you guys might be short on equipment," began Dr. Steele as he looked toward third base.

"No sir," mumbled Albert Hoye. The sun glinted off the blackberry jam dripping from Albert's mouth. "Just got us a half dozen balls."

"Bats are taped," piped June (short for Junior) Kendall using both hands to brush away crumbs from his shirt front, talking to no one I could see. "So we're ready."

Rufus Steele raised his chin and nodded toward the hound that by now lay flat, his nose busily sniffing at the bag, the ends of his ears collecting red dirt around home plate. Dr. Steele shrugged lightly, shifted his hat and squinted against the sun. "Guess I heard wrong."

Silence occupied the bench as our feet shuffled uneasily beneath it.

I gulped the last of my sandwich and stood to face my teammates. "We sure could use a catcher's mitt. Orval's grumbled about it more than once."

"True enough, Henry, that mitt was bad last season," Orval agreed readily.

"'Fraid there's no catcher's mitt, but you're welcome to have a look at the rest of it," offered Dr. Steele, motioning lazily back toward the bag.

I followed him at a distance, noting the dull yellowed letters WVU on the side of the bag as he unzipped the top and stepped back.

"You play ball?" I questioned.

"Used to," he replied, "a while back—with my brother."

By that time, the rest of the team had joined us around the bag. Sticky hands reached in to handle the expert array of well-used gloves, balls, and bats.

"Gosh darn, this dusty old slugger says 1924," hollered Albert, "When did you use it last?"

Rufus Steele got that strange look in his eye I'd seen several times before. Eventually, he answered softly, "Oh, about seven years ago; right, Old Bill?"

Alerted, the dog stared up at his master and held his gaze for a moment. Then his black eyes blinked, he exhaled softly, and sank back down in the dirt, watching the boys rummage carelessly through the equipment bag. When we began to throw the balls around, the dog gave a yowling whimper and took one from the bag. The ball quickly disappeared within his long jowls until just a slight bulge and a long slobber gave away its presence. Then he dropped the ball carefully on the ground between his big paws and began to lick its cover.

Dr. Steele reached down and gently scratched the dog's wrinkled head. "Old Bill's bein' possessive. He spent a lot of time chasing those balls. Right, boy?"

"You sure you're givin' all this stuff away?" June high-pitched the end of his question. "It looks mighty fine." Our best hitter, June couldn't resist the smooth length of the 32-inch bat. He rubbed his hands in the dirt, closed them around the big bat and swung it out from his right shoulder pretending to connect with a home run ball.

Rufus Steele puckered his lips and slowly rubbed the space between his lower lip and chin. He stared hard at the equipment that now lay scattered around home plate. "As I said, hasn't been used in a good long while. No need for it to go to waste. If you boys want any of it, it's yours. Looks like Old Bill would be grateful for that ball."

So intent were we on touching and smelling the delicious balls and bats, we forgot our manners. Dr. Steele was halfway to Maple Street before we remembered them. Wearing a glove on each hand, Orval and I loped after him to utter our thanks for his generous gifts.

"What position do you play?" I asked eagerly. "And your brother, what's he play?"

Dr. Steele paused, "We both played the outfield, me in center, Ronnie in right. He was the better hitter, but I could chase down a fly ball faster."

"How come you quit?" I continued. "Bet you can still play better than most. How about your brother? You sure he's okay sayin' good-bye to that equipment?"

"I'm sure," answered Rufus Steele, his shoulders sagging slightly. Touching the brim of his hat to signal his departure, he shifted his eyes and turned away.

Chapter Ten

It wasn't far, just through Dixon's cow pasture and across the dirt road where the narrow path began. Up we climbed for nearly an hour, scrambling hand over foot up the final stretch, until we came to the top of the hill, to stand beside the towering hickory trees, branches bending in the strong wind. Down to the east, we could see the remains of Fred Fox's enormous horse barn, burned to its foundation by a fire nearly eight years ago. As a boy, my father longed to ride the beautiful Percherons Mr. Fox raised in that barn. Luckily, Mr. Fox's dappled gray workhorses had all been sold off years before when the horse business began to fade in these parts.

We interrupted two deer feeding at a clump of chokecherry bushes. They broke cover and raced towards the east, away from the course of the storm, their tails white in retreat. A family of rabbits started as we passed under the trees, disappearing one by one into their burrow.

Knowing the squall would hit before we made it back down the steep path, we searched for shelter from the coming downpour. A shallow ravine revealed itself to our left, and I hollered through the wind to Woodrow to run in that direction. Together, we dived into a narrow opening just as the heavy rain arrived.

"I reckon this could be the back of that shaft," huffed Woodrow, heaving a few large stones from the entrance so he could squeeze inside. The small space was just large enough for two gangly boys if we crouched close together.

Earlier that morning, our fathers had instructed us to search out a coal mine shaft on the side of this hill, left vacant more than twenty years ago when a mining company abandoned it for an unknown reason. As teenagers hunting deer, Andrew and Frank Murphy discovered the shaft. The mine was old and had been worked for many years, but they believed there was plenty of coal left for the next few winters. As they explained, the entrance was partially blocked by rocks and timbers. Neither man was entirely clear on its exact location, but they figured we could at least exclude some parts of the hill from further searching. As it happened, the rain not only delayed our assignment; it produced an unexpected turn.

In the narrow dry space, Woodrow and I sat, elbows on our knees facing in opposite directions, backsides touching. I shifted slightly to rearrange a few rocks under my left buttocks. With an open hand, I touched the wall above my head to gauge the height of our small cave and judged it too low for anything but crawling or kneeling.

"Wonder how long this rain'll be." I spat on the floor a few feet in front of me.

"What d'you care? I don't," snapped Woodrow.

"You never care." I blurted, surprising myself.

"A lot you know," answered Woodrow.

"What did I do wrong?" I asked.

"Nothin'," he said.

"Nothin'?" I knew there had to be more than he was saying.

"Nothin'. You're just Henry Murphy. Henry Murphy. You can't help it." In a high-pitched taunt, he repeated my name. "I'm just Woodrow Murphy." His own name came out flat and angry. He picked up a pebble and threw it hard against the short dark wall of our cave. I ducked.

I sat for a minute wondering what to say next, but couldn't think of anything useful. So we listened to the rain splattering against the rocks outside and smelled its heavy metallic scent. I didn't exactly know what Woodrow was thinking, but I was startin' to put my finger on it.

"You're not still mad about that church play, are you?" I asked.

"No."

I tried again. "How 'bout that baseball game?"

"Not that either."

"What then?" Tired of guessing games, I closed my eyes hoping for the answer so this discussion would end.

"Ever' thing."

"Every thing?"

"Yeah, ever' thing." Woodrow sounded pretty definite.

Those words lay between us for awhile as Woodrow continued hurling pebbles at the wall.

I twisted my neck and shoulders around enough to see the pitiful look on Woodrow's face. Woodrow dropped his throwing hand and stared at me with his right eye. He began to talk.

"The day you were born, you were smart, strong, and could strike out three batters in a row. Day I came out, I was small, ugly, and dropped three easy pop flies. Like I said, you can't help it. But my life'd be a whole lot better if you weren't around." That said, Woodrow bolted from our small enclosure out into the rain. Without another word or backward glance, he rushed head first down the hillside.

Stunned by Woodrow's sudden leaving, I waited for the rain to stop. I used my pocket knife to dig a few chunks of what I thought was coal, out of the wall to show my father. Absently, I stuck them in my pocket and crawled out into the sunlight. I picked my way slowly down the path, thinking hard and stopping occasionally to collect a handful of hickory nuts. In truth, I was both surprised and puzzled by Woodrow's words. Try as I might, I couldn't figure out what had just passed between us, but I knew it wasn't good. While we were never the best of friends, I guess I'd always taken my cousin Woodrow for granted. Close in age, we'd been in the same school and Sunday school class our whole lives. Our families sometimes ate Sunday dinner together. We both worked hard, Woodrow harder than most because of his father's dairy farm. In summer, we both went swimming at Buffalo Bridge and fishing in the creek near Walter Wakefield's place. Heck, Woodrow was Woodrow. He was right about one thing, though. He wasn't much of a ballplayer. That other big sin I committed happened the day that Woodrow, playing left field, misjudged and overran a line drive, allowing three runs to score in the bottom of the last inning. His error cost us the game and almost the division championship that season. In an inexcusable violation of sportsmanship, I spit in his direction and stomped off without shaking his hand. Indeed, it was a terrible betrayal, and

I was ashamed of it; but I never found the courage to apologize. I thought about doing it now, convinced that particular offense was a major part of our problem. But, if it wasn't, I didn't want to make Woodrow feel worse, or add to his list of complaints against me, by bringing up old news. Or, maybe I was still a coward. Arguing with myself has never been easy.

Throughout most of my afternoon shift at the store, I worried. I reweighed Mrs. McConnell's buckwheat flour order twice and handed her the wrong amount of change from the register. Later, I knew I was thinking too hard about Woodrow's words when Junior Kendall got two home runs off me at practice. By the end of the season, hardly anybody could hit my fastball.

Before supper, my father inquired about the results of our morning climb up the hill. Transferring four lumps of coal from my pocket to the kitchen countertop (I knew better than to place them anywhere near the supper table); I described the ravine, the small cave, and Woodrow's notion that it could be the back of the main abandoned shaft. After he examined the coal lumps, my father agreed.

"Can you follow the back of that shaft for any distance?" he asked.

"Maybe, but only on your knees," I explained the low height of the cave and that I hadn't noticed any tunnels shooting off from it.

"After your last baseball game on Saturday, you can spend a lot more time on it," he ordered. "We've got to find that fuel source for the winter. September's nearly here with frost close behind. You and Woodrow need to find that main opening."

For any number of reasons, I didn't like the sound of that, and I suspected Woodrow wouldn't either.

After supper that night I tried to put that mess with Woodrow out of my mind. Luckily, it was *Jack Armstrong* night. I love stories—in books and on the radio. One of my favorite times of day comes after supper when my parents, Jim and I (and Stanley when he's home) sit in the parlor listening to adventures on the radio. After my father hears the evening news, Jim and I are permitted to listen to one program each before my mother twists the dial to *The Gospel Music Hour*. Since I was ten years old, I've listened twice a week to *Jack Armstrong, All American Boy*, a 15-minute serial about a high school athlete named Jack Armstrong who travels the world with his Uncle Jim and his two friends, Billy and Betty, solving crimes in far away places. Their journeys make me hungry to explore the world as a crime fighter or, better yet, a foreign correspondent for a famous newspaper. Jim's favorite program is *The Lone Ranger* about a masked Texas Ranger and his Indian guide Tonto who ride around on their horses finding people to help and handing out silver bullets. The *Lone Ranger* stories are kind of predictable. Everyone wants to know the mystery behind the mask. We gather around close and get real quiet so we can hear the announcer as he proclaims in his familiar voice: "A fiery horse with the speed of light, a cloud of dust and a hearty "Hi-yo Silver." I never get tired of that announcer's voice. On alternate nights, my mother likes to listen to *The Kate Smith Hour*, especially when Miss Smith sings patriotic songs like *God Bless America*.

My favorite shows are all the adventure stories: *Superman, Sergeant Preston of the Yukon, Tom Mix.* Usually I like to hear the sound effects or to figure out which character is talking. Listening hard makes the story real, makes it spread out in my mind. Everything is quiet. We all sit in the parlor and stare at nothing in particular. Jim lays flat on the floor, belly up, both hands making a pillow under his head, looking intently at the ceiling. My mother rocks back and forth in her flowered rocking chair, twiddling her thumbs, closing her eyes or staring at the busy hands in her lap. Used to a lifetime of work, her hands are never still. Sometimes, she knits or darns our socks as she sings along with Kate Smith. My father sits next to the furnace in his big black rocker, tapping his foot, gazing at the light from the kerosene lamp as it flickers on the wall. My eyes stare out the window or at the upright piano with all our pictures on top, but I see nothing except the story's action in my head. Tonight, however, I wasn't listening to the story. I was replaying that situation with Woodrow and wondering what I could do to set things right.

Chapter Eleven

The following month, September 1939, brought two dark catastrophes into our home. The first involved a war on the other side of the world, the second a mine shaft on the other side of our hill.

On Sunday night, September 3, my family gathered around the parlor radio to listen to the latest of President Roosevelt's fireside chats. Home for supper, Stanley brought with him two new batteries which he and my father quickly installed before the broadcast began. Recent discussions in the general store had focused on the threat of invasions in Europe, and we expected the president's comments to include some mention of them. We were not prepared, however, for the serious announcement on this particular night. The radio crackled. My father reached a long arm to turn the knob up higher as Mr. Roosevelt began, ". . . I had hoped against hope that some miracle would prevent a devastating war in Europe and bring to an end the invasion of Poland by Germany . . . which is today unhappily a fact."

For the next ten minutes, the president talked about facts and rumors and other nations where peace no longer existed. While I did not understand everything Mr. Roosevelt said, like my parents and Stanley, I felt great relief at his ending remarks, "I hope the United States will keep out of this war. I believe that it will."

We all sat motionless. My parents were old enough to remember the last big war in Europe, the one that killed thousands of soldiers, many of them Americans. I looked up to see my mother looking intently at Stanley before she invited us all to hold hands and offer up a prayer for peace on earth. We feared that bombs would begin to drop from the sky.

Two days later, on Tuesday afternoon at the general store, neighbors were still talking about the unsettling news. I hurried in after school and began to put on my work apron. Uncle Frank and my father stood talking with Ray McConnell. Out of the corner of my eye, I spotted Woodrow leaning against the back counter. We had not seen each other since that day on the hill, and tension rose between us when our eyes met.

"Hold on, Henry," said my father. "You and Woodrow have another assignment this afternoon. Before dark, head on up the other side of the hill and see if you two can find that coal shaft." He reached behind the register counter and pulled out a small lantern. "Take this with you. It's filled and ready." He threw me a box of matches that I tucked quickly into my shirt pocket. "Woodrow's got a lantern and a couple lengths of chalk to mark your path once you get inside."

Uncle Frank instructed, "Watch out for critters in those old shafts and snakes that go in after 'em. Can't use a shotgun; vibration might cause a cave-in. You both know better 'n to mess with ladders or step in water. Just find the seam; we'll do the rest."

Heads down, Woodrow and I reached the screen door at the same time. I stepped aside and let him pass first. Before I could walk through, the door sprung back and hit the edge of my lantern, almost shattering the glass cover. By the time I adjusted it, Woodrow was halfway down Maple Street, and I ran to catch up.

We knew we were looking for the mouth to an old wagon mine, most likely hidden by grass or heavy brush. Steadily, we climbed the opposite side of the hill from where we took shelter in the small cave. By 4:00, we were two-thirds of the way up the side.

Woodrow and I stood on a high knoll about fifty yards below the top of the hill and studied the rocky slope. Aside from a few grunts we had not exchanged words that afternoon, and although we'd both walked to the same place, we had not walked together.

Woodrow pointed, "Catch that clump of thorny locust bushes up the hill a piece? I reckon that's it."

"Could be; let's see what's back there," I agreed.

Slowed somewhat by the lanterns attached to our waist belts, we made our way along a narrow ledge that ended about ten feet above the locust bushes. Looking down, we spied a stack of old timbers and a pattern of rocks that seemed to lead further on. We slid and stumbled hard down the slope until we reached a flat wide surface which could easily have been used as a wagon loading area years before. We cut through the knee-high grass (thigh-high on Woodrow) and stepped over the old lumber, careful not to disturb any hidden snakes. I never held much affection for timber rattlers. Sure enough, an opening, hidden by a larger locust bush, showed itself in front of us. As soon as we recognized the mouth of the mine, we sized up its width and height and decided I could step inside without bending much more than my head and shoulders. Woodrow just needed to bend his knees a bit. Lean and wiry, he could slip easily through the arched opening with no trouble at all. We looked at each other and both shrugged in agreement as we undid the lanterns from our belts. Heeding Uncle Frank's advice, we examined the entryway for critters and decided it was safe to look around. Once inside, the opening widened out. When our eyes adjusted to the light, we found ourselves at the top of a narrow tunnel that sloped downwards into the hillside. For a moment, I was reminded of the rabbit hole in *Alice in Wonderland*, a book we read last month in Mrs. Early's English class. Of all my teachers, she would have appreciated my memory of that detail. In fact, it was the one detail in the book that interested me since I wasn't much taken with tea parties and wicket games and such.

Lighting our lanterns with the same match, I sensed that both Woodrow and I hoped for a quick look, a coal seam nearby to pick a few good nuggets and a speedy trip back down the hill to supper. Unfortunately, as we leaned in opposite directions to search the walls with the lantern light, no obvious coal seam appeared in this outer entrance where we stood.

"Nothing I can see. How 'bout your side?" I began.

"Nope, no luck here," said Woodrow. "Have to go further in."

While neither of us seemed keen on spending a lot of time in that shaft, we never once thought of being in any danger. By the time we learned different it was too late.

Carrying the lantern in my right hand, I went in first. Woodrow followed with his own lantern on the left, so he could use his right hand to rub a chalk line along the middle of the wall. Like dropping bread crumbs in the woods, the white mark was meant to make sure we could find our way back to the opening. Coal mines are full of tunnels, cross cuts and small picking rooms. Without a clearly marked trail, it's easy enough to take a wrong turn and get lost.

I sniffed the stale air. It smelled like a shed that had been closed up for awhile. The word "rusty" didn't quite describe it, but came close, reminding me of an old tractor sitting too long in the rain. We set off along the rutted path, bordered on both sides by a water-filled ditch. Small puddles filled the path's ruts, and we stepped around or over them so our shoes stayed dry. We walked on a slight downhill grade, the light from the opening disappearing slowly as we continued in. In the distance, the faint sound of dripping water signaled the source of the ditch water. About 50 yards on, a trickle ran down the dark wall and seeped steadily into the ditch. Our own footsteps echoed down the shaft. I jumped at the sound of flapping wings, raising my free hand to shield my face in case of a swooping bat—that never came. Lamps held high, we silently inspected two small rooms off the main tunnel. In one room, an old pick lay on the ground, left, I guessed, from a miner's last job. Finding nothing that looked promising, we moved down the tunnel. I was aware of the increasing darkness as Woodrow's lantern sputtered and died, limiting our vision. He stood rock-still, hardly breathing, while I fished the matches from my shirt pocket and relit it quickly. The match crushed under Woodrow's foot. We heard rocks fall to the ground, but couldn't tell how many or how near they might be. Further, we came upon a group of props, a thick forest of dense poles holding back the ground above us. Confused by their long shadows, we stopped, unsure of where we were or how far we'd come.

"We still walkin' straight in? How many rooms we passed?" I turned to hear Woodrow's ghostly voice, glad to hear something besides the slow-burning kerosene in my lantern and the hollowness of our footsteps. The lantern sat on the ground between us.

"Don't know; I *think* we've come in a straight line. I haven't been counting the rooms or cross cuts. You?" I asked, hoping the sweat on my forehead did not show.

"Nah. Wish we had more light; I can't see too much," replied Woodrow.

With dampness all around, the air was heavy. There was an uneasy buzz in my head, and I shook myself to clear it. When my foot slipped on an up-turned shovel that lay beside the path, a chill swept through my body. I felt a sudden need to turn back, to run toward the opening, to make sure it still existed, that I could step outside into the light. But, in fourteen years, I'd never disobeyed my father's instructions. Neither would I disappoint him. We needed this coal. I didn't want to be in this black hole, but I'd do what needed to be done. I took a deep breath and continued on, relieved to feel Woodrow a few steps behind. As far as I knew, he might feel the same way, just keeping it to himself, like I was.

"Woodrow, you OK?"

"Guess so," he mumbled as he bore down hard on another white mark on the wall.

We held our lamps higher and peered hopefully into the blackness. The gloom seemed to lighten when we came to a spot where the track widened out. A dark vein about the width of a fence rail ran vertically up the wall on our right, wriggling out here and there at its sides. Woodrow recognized it, too.

"Dig out a few rocks here," he said setting aside the chalk and pulling his knife from his pocket. "Shine me some light on it, and let's get outta here."

I moved around a few feet ahead of him until the lamp cast the widest and brightest light on the spot where he worked. Pressing one hand against the rock, Woodrow made four deep cuts in the vein. Since I was just standing there waiting, I figured now was as good a time as any to spit out that apology I owed him. I took a breath and licked my lips to call up some courage. With my free hand, I pretended to crank up the lantern knob so as not to look straight at him.

"You, uh, uh, you ever think about that baseball game when you played the outfield? The one we, uh, lost in the last inning?" I stammered.

Woodrow lowered his blackened fingers and placed the jagged lump of coal in his pocket. Head tilted away from the light, his eyes narrowed when he looked at me. "What are you gettin' at?"

I cleared my throat, "Just wonderin', I did something that day I'm none too pr . . ."

Before I finished the sentence, a great force knocked my legs from under me and hurled me backwards against the wall. Rocks fell like rain. I watched Woodrow's image disappear, replaced by buckling props falling in upon themselves. A huge thunder overwhelmed me as the earth collapsed upon us. I landed on my back, hard enough to drive the wind out of me. My arms spread wide as I fell. I couldn't breathe. I lay there against the wall, stunned, until the noise stopped. What stretch of time passed, I don't know. Rocks, big and small, jumbled in heaps. My face was covered by a thick layer of dust, clogging my nose, clinging to my eyes, and filling my ears. Propping myself up on an elbow, I snorted and spit dirt and pebbles from my nose and mouth, coughing and struggling for every breath. I wiped dirt from my eyes, trying to focus through the fog and sudden darkness. I realized the lantern was buried beneath the rocks. Panicked, I tried hard not to be afraid. Concentrating, I heard its sizzle and moved toward the sound, desperate to restore the light. The smell of kerosene led me to it. As my hands closed on the warm round cylinder, I offered up a prayer that it would light. Shakily, I reached into my pocket and fumbled for the match box as my eyes grew more accustomed to the darkness.

As pain split my chest, I called out hoarsely, "Woodrow, can you hear me?" My words bounced back at me, and I had a sensation of being utterly alone.

At last, a match stick rose between my fingers. I struck it blindly across the wall, and the match flame burst to life. I held the lantern in close, winding the small knob in what I hoped was the right direction. The match flickered slightly against it before the wick hissed with light. Pulling myself up amidst the dirt, rocks, and splintered posts and turning slowly around, my heart dropped when I saw that I was completely surrounded by a wall of rock with no clear way through, at least none that I could see.

With full breath in my lungs, I hollered, "Woodrow, Woodrow" before I collapsed in a fit of pain and coughing. Sound filled the narrow room. I struggled to listen.

A muffled voice came to me through the wall. Moving in its direction, I hollered back to let him know

I'd heard something. I set the lantern on a fallen prop and pulled out a rock halfway up the wall. Reassured at how easily it came loose, I reached hastily for another.

Maybe I could move enough rocks to crawl through to the other side.

Without warning, more rocks hurtled down upon me. Ducking, I wrenched my shirt around my head and quickly grabbed the lantern before flattening myself against the far wall. Afraid of another collapse, I stood very still, hoping I'd survive this second cave-in. After a few seconds, pebbles settled at my feet, and silence resumed. I leaned against the wall, panting and sweating like a damp old dog. I inhaled a painful breath and called out, "Woodrow, can you hear me?"

He did not reply. I listened for a long time. I feared my luck was running out.

Chapter Twelve

Shivering with pain and fright, I knew I was trapped. My breath came harder and harder. I bit my lip, tasting dirt and soot—like the last ashes of a campfire—in my mouth. I searched the ground for water, desperate for a puddle to show itself, however foul the water might be.

I told myself I was not lost, that my life was not over.

I began to worry about Woodrow, whether he was hurt or trapped in some small place like the one I was in. Again, I called out with no reply. My mind raced through possibilities. Maybe he escaped the sliding rocks. Maybe he ran back to the entrance. Maybe he'll bring help. Maybe he lay under a heap of timber and earth. Before the second cave-in, I heard a voice on the other side of this wall. At that time, then, he was alive—enough to talk, to yell or moan. But nothing after the second cave-in, not a sound.

This can't be happening. I'm going to wake up now in the creaky bed I share with Jim, him lying sprawled across the bottom, like always. My mother's going to holler upstairs now for us to get dressed and do our chores before breakfast, like always. My bare feet are going to hit the cold floor now as I fling off the cover and stretch out my arms, like always.

With eyes closed, carefully, I went through each motion; I imagined my mother's call and Jim's sleepy head. I willed myself to stay in that safe place. But when my eyes opened, I stood in the middle of my small dark room listening to the crackle of the kerosene lantern, watching my shadow on the wall.

Finally, I said aloud, "I am not trapped in a hot, dark coal mine with no way out. I'm not. I'm not. Please tell me I'm not."

And why, why should I be here?
I was just doing what my father ordered.
I was just being a good son, doing what he told me.
Just trying to keep my family warm for the winter.
Why should I be the one who had to do this job?
It wasn't fair, sending me up here with Woodrow—who hates me anyway.
Most likely, he's run off and is just gonna leave me here.
He said he'd be better off if I weren't around.
He said that.
Now he got his wish.

I picked up a pebble at my feet and threw it sidearm against the opposite wall, hard enough to bounce back and smack the lantern. I resolved to be more careful. At that moment, the lantern and the matches in my pocket were the two most important, if not the only, items I possessed.

I couldn't be too hard on Woodrow. If I'd had courage enough to apologize or good sense enough not to have acted a fool about a silly baseball game, I might not be in this mess. Last Sunday's sermon, the preacher talked about reaping what you sow. Guess that's what was happening to me right now. Unfair? Maybe, but taking things out on Woodrow wasn't the answer, especially since I didn't know where he was or what condition he was in. Could be, he was worse off than I was. I sure hoped he'd gotten out of this tunnel and run at least halfway back down the hill by now.

"OK, let's figure this out," I said to no one but myself and the lantern.

As calmly as I could manage, I stated aloud the order of things that had to happen to get me out of this place, picturing each event in my mind, much like our evening radio programs.

"If Woodrow's all right, he could make it back to the mouth of the shaft in about 20 minutes—if he had his lantern and found the trail markers.

"From the opening, he could make it down the hill in about 30 minutes—if he wasn't hurt bad.

"When he got to the bottom of the hill, he could catch a ride to town to fetch my father, or up to Uncle Frank's dairy barn to get Uncle Frank.

"Together, they'd have to get shovels and lights and such and climb back up the hill, into the shaft, and down the tunnel.

"That's pretty near two hours before any digging could start—if it's safe to work the tunnel."

I reckoned there were a whole lot of "ifs" in that story, but it was all I had. I worried the kerosene would last even two hours. To my way of thinking, that was the least amount of time I would be imprisoned in this place. What could I do in the meantime? I'd go crazy just sitting here. I started reciting the multiplication tables, but that didn't take long and wasn't real interesting, same with state capitals. I recalled a few psalms like the twenty-third, which I thought was fitting in this situation. Those words brought me some degree of comfort. Last spring for our poetry unit, Mrs. Early made us memorize *Paul Revere's Ride*, all 130 lines of it. I repeated it aloud, using the lantern as my audience, exaggerating the march of the grenadiers, the crowing of the cock, the barking of the farmer's dog. As I chanted the final lines, I shook my fist dramatically in the dusty air,

> *"For, borne on the night-wind of the Past,*
> *Through all our history, to the last,*

*In the hour of darkness and peril and need,
The people will waken and listen to hear
The hurrying hoof beats of that steed,
And the midnight message of Paul Revere."*

When she assigned that homework task, I grumbled about it and surely spent too much time for what it was worth. But, sure enough, Mrs. Early was right again. She said that poem would come in real handy for us in the future and that we'd always remember it.

On my own, I had memorized *Casey at the Bat*. It was the first poem about sports I'd ever read. I loved the highs and lows of it, both in suspense and rhyme. I didn't know what some of the words meant, but they sounded real fine in that poem.

"But there is no joy in Mudville: Mighty Casey has struck out." I swung through the pitch with my imaginary bat and felt a sharp pain rattle through my chest.

I was running out of poems, leastwise ones I could remember all the way through. My mouth was dry, and not much time was passing, far as I could tell.

Doubts worried my mind.

No one's coming.

The tunnel's blocked.

No one knows where the shaft is except Woodrow and me.

It will be dark soon.

As my fears mounted, the walls grew taller and drew closer in. Crawling into a corner, I made myself small, a circle of comfort, crouching with my head on my knees. At some point, I put my arms down and stared at nothing but the black shadows.

What's the worst thing that could happen?

I chose not to dwell on it, but needed to have that likelihood out of the way.

What's the best thing that could happen?

A lantern to light the way home.

Home in time for supper: potatoes, beans, biscuits, and fresh fish with blueberry pie for dessert.

Fishing in my pants pocket, I felt a bit of maple candy, fuzzy with old lint. Desperate to relieve the bitter taste of dirt, I sucked hard on the tiny scrap and unexpectedly discovered what starving people already knew: When required, you eat anything at hand. It was a lesson I needed to learn.

Time passed slowly. I counted backwards from a thousand. I listed all the goods my father sold at the general store and their shelf number. I recited all the presidents up to Mr. Franklin Roosevelt, although I missed a few after General Grant and before Mr. Teddy Roosevelt.

My fears rose again as I struggled to breathe and the lantern began to sputter. I wondered how much air was left in the room. After a time, I began to lose hope and drifted into a light sleep, my head nodding forward against my chest.

Jerking awake, I sat straight up and listened hard for the smallest sound. Straining to hold my breath, I heard a thump, then a scrape like something sliding on the floor.

There it was again, the same pattern: thump and scrape, thump and scrape.

No, it was just my imagination, a dream.

Now, there's nothing.

I only saw the thing out of the corner of my eye. A section of the wall above me quivered. Fearing another cave-in, I moved quickly toward the now dimly-burning lantern. Almost at the same moment, I heard a noise, louder now, but the same thump and scrape as before.

Hopefully, I called out, "Can anybody hear me? Is anybody out there?"

A short, muffled reply came in return, then a longer one, neither of which I could understand. I hollered louder, "It's me. It's Henry. I'm trapped."

Once more, the roof above me trembled, and I backed away, clutching the lantern's handle, thankful that someone had come to my rescue, but fearful the roof would fall in upon me.

The thumping and scraping continued until finally I heard a familiar voice.

"Henry, can you hear me? Are you hurt?"

"I can hear you, Dr. Steele. I'm hurt, but not too bad, I reckon. What about Woodrow?"

"Woodrow tore up his arm pretty bad, but he wouldn't let me tend it. He told me where to find you and went to get more help and more light. This lantern won't last too much longer," he said.

"Mine either," I agreed, "It's almost gone. Not sure if it's the kerosene or the air."

"Stand up, Henry," Dr. Steele shouted. "Don't sit down. There's bad air near the floor. And don't move around too much so as not to stir it up. How long you been in there?"

"Don't rightly know. Woodrow and I started into the tunnel near four o'clock. What time is it now?" I asked, my head swimming as I stood in place.

"Nearly seven. Put your shirt over your nose and mouth and don't breathe in too much. It's a little late for that now, but better to be safer from here on," he warned. As he talked, I heard the steady thump and scrape in the background. More than once, I sensed the rocks moving beneath my feet and saw the shadows tremble on the wall. Suddenly, a shower of stones rained down from the roof above me.

Terrified, I put up my hands and screamed, "Stop, stop digging. You're making it worse; it's all coming down."

I feared that if one more rock was pulled from the fragile wall, the whole of it would collapse and fall. The more I thought of it and imagined it, the more disturbed and scared I became. I ranted, crazy with fear, shouting words I do not remember at Dr. Steele. But it held. The walls stopped moving. Everything was still. The next moment my lantern sputtered and slowly flickered out, blackening my small world and adding to my desperation. I panted for air and self-control.

"Dr. Steele, my lantern just died. Everything's black, and I'm as good as blind."

In a gentle positive voice, Rufus Steele answered, "It's all right, Henry. My mother used to say, 'On the darkest night, you can see the stars.' Can you see the stars, Henry?"

"I, uh, it's, uh, I'm trying, Dr. Steele. I'm trying real hard. I can't decide," I gasped.

"It's not something you decide, Henry," he said thoughtfully, then added in a stern voice, "This is what's going to happen now. My lantern will soon be out, so we have to take a risk and keep digging on this side. Otherwise, we'll both be trapped here in the dark. Because we can hear each other, that means I'm pretty close to you now. In just a minute or two, you should be able to see the light of my lantern. Hold on, and be ready to crawl quickly through any opening you see. Just keep coming through; don't stop."

I had to trust Rufus Steele. Once again, I thought of the worst thing that could happen and the best thing that could happen. My eyes looked up toward the roof.

"I see 'em, Dr. Steele. I reckon there's hundreds of 'em. Your mother was right," I declared loudly.

A hearty chuckle floated through the wall. "She always was, Henry; she always was."

There was hardly a second between the last thump and scrape and the glimmer of light that shone through a small opening in my prison wall. At once, I was down on my knees fighting through rocks, pushing hard through the dirt, moving instinctively in the direction of the light. Two large hands twisted my body and lifted me up, throwing me forward away from the crumbling wall.

"No time to waste, Henry, keep moving. I've got the lantern and the shovel. I'm right behind you," urged my rescuer.

I stumbled blindly up the path as my eyes readjusted to the light. Everything was a shade of black. A deep rumble vibrated behind me, and I shuddered as I heard the wall seal itself once again. Thankfully, I felt Rufus Steele close on my heels.

When we had run a distance, I turned to face Dr. Steele. Doing my best to act confident beyond what I felt and keep my voice from shaking, I said, "I'm much obliged to you, Dr. Steele. That's the third time you've saved a member of my family." That wasn't exactly what I meant, but it came out close enough.

"Not a problem, Henry, not a problem. Far as I recall, it was you and Jim saved your brother Stanley's life. I just patched him up after you'd done the hard part. Now let's move before this light expires, or you'll be taking back that measure of thanks."

Chapter Thirteen

When it happened I was up the shaft a ways counting the number of matches we had between us. In the bowl of my two hands lay our measly back-up plan. Seventeen small wooden matches—three from my shirt pocket and fourteen from Rufus Steele's—meant we might be able to find Woodrow's trail markers, even in a pitch black tunnel. I had replaced the last match into my pocket when, for the second time that day, my world went completely dark.

"Stay put, Henry. Don't move an inch. We knew this might come about. How many matches we got?"

"Seventeen, sir. Don't reckon that'll help much."

"Keep talking, Henry. I don't want to pass you by. You're holding our way outta here."

"How's that? These seventeen matches will last us about eighteen seconds."

Before his arm touched my shoulder, I knew Rufus Steele now stood directly alongside me. "Never cared much for the dark, always left me scared a little," he said casually.

"That makes two of us," I agreed, not realizing I had just learned one of the few pieces of information I would ever know about Rufus Steele.

"What happened to your brother?" I risked asking. It was an answer I'd wanted for some time.

There was a long silence; so long I thought I'd gone too far in my curiosity.

"He's dead, died in a smallpox outbreak seven years ago in the Tennessee Valley. Unlike you, Henry, I couldn't save my brother. I tried, but not soon enough—or hard enough," he added softly.

"That why you gave us that baseball equipment?" I questioned.

"It was time," he said. "Funny conversation to be having in the middle of this place, isn't it?" He put one arm around my shoulders and held it there for a moment. I sensed he needed something to hold onto as much as I did. "Maybe we'll both make it out of a dark tunnel tonight.

"You're the math wizard, Henry. We've got 17 dry matches. Any idea how far we need to walk to reach the opening?"

"Near as I remember, Woodrow and I walked about twenty minutes in, but we were looking for coal veins and such and marking our trail, so we made pretty slow time. That means you and me could walk for about a minute, then light a match and check for a marker," my voice rose at the end of the sentence to make sure Rufus Steele agreed with my suggestion.

Out of fear or sound judgment, neither of us had moved our position. That meant we were still facing in the direction we needed to head.

"Your timing sounds good, Henry, but we've got to know we haven't passed a marker or taken a cross cut by mistake. If we get going down the wrong cut, we're lost. We've got to keep our bearings so we don't get turned around. It's easy to do in here. If I knew the air was good, I'd say we ought to stay where we are and wait for a proper rescue," warned Rufus Steele.

"No," I argued. "I can't wait here in the dark, neither one of us. I won't let you."

As my chest squeezed with pain, I thought hard how to convince Rufus Steele to start moving. I put my hands out at waist level and moved them outward until they'd completed a circle of my body. Taking a step sideways, my left foot splashed ankle-deep into the water ditch, soaking my shoe and sock. I regained my balance and found my target, touching my fingertips against the tunnel wall. "I know how we can do it. I'll brush my fingers along the wall as we walk. We'll keep close together. Every minute or so, we'll use a match to find the marker."

I waited for some kind of response, certain that Rufus Steele would not trust my strategy.

"You put it that way, Henry, it's purely possible, purely possible," he said. "Let's strike our first match and see where we are."

Sure enough, a white mark, hurriedly but clearly scribbled, showed itself about a third of the way up the rough wall not more than 20 feet from where we stood. The match burned away. My fingers found the wall. We each set the clock inside our heads and moved awkwardly along our invisible path, listening to the regular squish of my now heavy left shoe and wondering if we would make it. I had to believe we had a chance.

After about thirty seconds Rufus Steele said, "Let me tell you about the last baseball game I played, Henry. I'll give it to you pitch by pitch." And so he did, in his strong distinctive voice, following behind me with his hand upon my shoulder.

I reckon it would have seemed a little strange to most people to encounter two blind young men limping their way through the darkness, one describing a lazy line drive to center field, a catcher crouching, willing his pitcher to fling a pure fastball or crafty slider across the plate; the other staring ahead into the blackness but picturing each account, eager for the next batter to swing and miss. Long about the fifth inning, we made our way up an angled slope and stopped. Knowingly, we lit our final match and strode forward searching hopefully for the white mark Woodrow would have placed. As the match and a sliver of hope faded in my fingers, the light of the moon's last quarter surprised us. Framed by the arch of the tunnel's entrance, it was surrounded by thousands of stars.

Had it not been for the perilous nature of it, I would have described that journey as both remarkable and wonderful.

Chapter Fourteen

Over the next few weeks our broken bodies—Woodrow's left hand and my three ribs—healed themselves. During that time, we spent a fair amount of time together, and I learned the order and circumstances by which Woodrow and Dr. Steele saved my life. Late one afternoon, as we sat around a rough wooden table on the pantry porch snapping beans for supper and drinking sassafras tea, Woodrow explained, as best he could remember, the events I did not know. Jim sat on the edge of the porch, legs dangling over the new batch of kittens huddled together in the dirt. He finished whittling a new whistle and listened intently to the story of my rescue.

After the first collapse, Woodrow found himself facedown wedged among half a dozen thick props. Once he realized I wasn't in sight, he started hollering and trying to dig me out. A large boulder struck his hand, flattening most of his fingers and breaking the knuckles, when the second cave-in happened. It was then he grabbed the lantern and ran for help, figuring my air would last for only a couple of hours or less. On his way down the hillside, he ran head long into Dr. Steele's coupe parked at Bud Barefoot's truck farm where the doctor was checking on Ginny Barefoot's new baby. That's when Dr. Steele directed Woodrow and Bud to find Andrew and Frank Murphy while he borrowed Bud's shovel and Woodrow's lantern and hurried to the mine shaft.

"I wasn't sure you had any interest in rescuing me; wouldn't blame you if you didn't," I said as I stared at the half-filled tea jar.

Woodrow wiped his mouth on his sleeve and squinted at me, "How's that?"

This time, I did not struggle for words. "Fact is, Woodrow, a couple of times, especially one no-account baseball game, I acted real bad towards you. I'm real sorry. I hope you'll forgive me. I thank you for saving my life. And if there's ever anything I can do for you . . ."

Before I finished my sentence, Woodrow's eyebrows rose clear up his forehead, his face broke into a wide grin, and his head bobbed up and down again and again. Excitedly, he blurted, "There sure is something, Henry. You can teach me to play baseball. Not pitcher or anything like you. But I'd be grateful if you'd teach me to play the outfield and hit a pitch or two so I could be on the team."

Now there was a tall order. I scratched my nose and whistled to myself, stalling for time, not wanting to let on how impossible that request might be. And the thought of persuading the other guys to let Woodrow play was another thing altogether. All the same, I'd made an offer, and now I was obliged to make good on it. For the sake of conversation, I asked earnestly, "Which field are you aiming to play, Woodrow?"

"I gave a strong consideration to right field, Henry. I'm not too good at left field, as you recall," he replied awkwardly, hanging his head at the still painful memory.

"Right field," I repeated, which set me to thinking. "Right field. You know Dr. Steele's brother played right field at the university. I bet Dr. Steele would help us out," hoping Rufus Steele could save my hide one more time.

That still left the hitting part to wrestle with. "Tell me the kind of pitches you can hit, Woodrow," I said.

"What do you mean, Henry, what kind of pitches?"

"You know—sliders, knuckleballs, curveballs, fastballs—different pitches thrown at batters," I explained, our chances for success sinking still further.

"None of 'em; I've never hit a ball pitched at me," Woodrow admitted sheepishly.

"Never?" I squeaked.

"Nope, never," Woodrow declared.

Yep, I thought, clearly this was going to be a very tall order. Luckily, baseball season did not start for another seven months.

Chapter Fifteen

The first Saturday in June 1940 attested to the crispness of Garrett County's summer days. Sweet smelling mountain air and clear blue sky made the perfect setting for our opening ballgame. A slight breeze drifted in from center field. It appeared as if half the town had set aside chores and church services for the afternoon. There were no empty seats in the thin wooden bleachers, and the street in front of the field was full of cars and wagons—from the train station down to Nicklow's Hotel. For shade, the women wore their sun bonnets, and the men their fishing caps, so both the visitors' and the home bleachers were busy with color. My mother and Jim sat in the middle of the top row along the third base line. I noticed Nancy Kendall and her friends nearby pointing at her brother, June, and giggling. One of them pointed at me while I practiced a few warm-up pitches.

In our successful run to last year's championship, we'd beaten the Markleysburg team twice, but we heard they'd got hold of a pitcher and a good clean-up hitter in the off-season. So, we weren't sure what to expect from their new line-up.

Our own team roster had changed little, with the exception of Ivan Early now sharing right field duties with Woodrow Murphy—on an as-needed basis, of course. I'd had to do some smooth talking and make some hard promises, especially to June Kendall and Albert Hoye, before the team would consider allowing Woodrow on the field, or the bench. He'd done pretty well in practice this week, catching routine balls in center and right fields, but I could tell the other guys were just waiting for an excuse to send him packing. For his own sake, I wanted Woodrow to play. But I wasn't sure if that meant losing my other teammates in the bargain.

For the last six months since his hand healed up, even in the dead of winter, Woodrow and I practiced two afternoons a week and for an hour every Saturday and Sunday with Rufus Steele. Mostly, we repeated throwing and catching the ball until Woodrow could shoot it back to me without much thought. I marked a tree target for Woodrow to aim at; we strung up a flat tire to a tree limb and endlessly pitched the ball through its opening. Mercilessly, Rufus Steele drove line drives at Woodrow until Woodrow's hand hurt, and then switched to pop flies and grounders. Finally, he had Woodrow running all over creation chasing down long fly balls. Watching Rufus Steele play ball, I knew he's been a mighty fine baseball player. He had an easy pair of hands and a smooth swing. He threw the ball with a long graceful motion. The way he tossed the ball in the air and leaned into his swing, his one-handed catches all made me believe there was more to the story than he was telling. Before each practice, we ran sprints up and down Maple Street. While it might sound like hard work, I never thought of it as such. Woodrow never complained, and I sure didn't. In fact, I looked forward to each practice session and silently thanked Woodrow for improving my game as well as his own. In the process, we found out Woodrow had a pretty good throwing arm, and he was a fairly fast fielder—even on his shorter legs.

Hitting was a different story. It didn't take long to discover that Woodrow had two problems. First, he had a clumsy swing, one that chopped its way through the ball. As much as we practiced, he never looked comfortable. Second, he took his eye off the ball. In fact, he even closed them when he saw the ball getting too close for his comfort. In any case, we worked hard all autumn and winter, and I was certain that Woodrow was a much better ball player, surely more consistent, than when we'd started. I knew he thought so too. Still, given his past experiences with the game, he didn't have much confidence.

I didn't give it much consideration when we took the field for the first inning of play as the three o'clock train whistled its way through the depot, and the umpire shouted "Play ball."

Two hours later, we found ourselves in an unlikely mess. In the bottom of the last inning, the game was on the line for the Friendsville nine. The score was two to four. We'd given up four runs—two in the seventh inning on a fly ball to right. The batter had walloped the ball hard. Racing full steam, Ivan misjudged it and the closeness of the right field drop-off. After the ball smacked him in the face, he tumbled down the hillside and sprained his ankle. In the time it took both his eye and his ankle to swell up, two runs scored. He had a lump above his left eye and couldn't walk, so his back-up, Woodrow Murphy, took Ivan's place in right field while he sat on the bench with one ice pack on his eye and another wrapped around his ankle.

As the teams changed places in the middle of the ninth inning, not one fan had left his seat. All remained hopeful for a win, a tribute to our usual record. Our batting line-up looked right enough for the bottom of the ninth. But before we knew it, our first hitter lined out to the shortstop, and the second sent up a pop foul to the catcher. Two outs with three runs needed to win, things looked bleak. Orval was on deck with Albert, Woodrow, and June following in the line-up. Of course, we all had our fingers crossed that June would get a chance to bat, but there seemed little likelihood of that. Then, on his third pitch, Orval connected with a clean single to short center. Albert took a fast walk to first base when the umpire called four balls in a row. Things were looking up with men on first and second. On deck, Woodrow fidgeted with the grip on his bat and chewed his lower lip. Nervously, he looked my way. I nodded, putting two fingers to my eyes to signal for him to keep his eyes open and on the ball. The crowd fell silent when Woodrow picked up a bat, swung through once and slowly advanced to the plate, head down.

On his last trip, the Markleysburg pitcher had served up three fastballs over the middle, and Woodrow had swung at and missed each one. This time, Rufus Steele, standing in the third base coach's box, was giving the signals. He swiped one sleeve, then the other and rested his hands on his hips for a brief moment before touching each shoulder in turn and sleeves again. It was the third signal that was real. Woodrow couldn't keep still. He cleared his throat and coughed, swirled his tongue around his lips, propped the bat against his leg, and wiped both palms down the front of his shirt. Finally, he stood in the batter's box, ready for the pitch. When the ball left the pitcher's hand, I could tell it was a curveball. Holding our breaths, the whole team saw the ball catch the outside corner of the plate.

"Strike one," shouted the ump, muffled in the padding of his mask. The crowd muttered and edged forward in their seats. The ump adjusted his mask for a better view. Woodrow eyed the third base coach's box. Once again, Rufus Steele gave the signal. I cupped my hands over my mouth and shouted encouragement, "Stand in there, Woodrow, you can do it."

Just as the pitcher was about to throw the next ball, Woodrow stepped out of the batter's box. The catcher looked up at him and sneered. I couldn't make out what he said, but I could guess it was meant to rattle Woodrow more than he already was. Meanwhile, the rest of the bench was staring at me. June's cheeks were puffed out to Sunday. I understood. Just for something to do, I leaned over and concentrated on lacing up my shoes real tight.

Rufus Steele walked around, rubbed his hands together, and hollered for Woodrow to loosen up. Woodrow stepped into the batter's box and took a deep breath. The catcher signaled to the pitcher; this time a fastball flew toward the plate. Woodrow watched it go by; the umpire's huge right hand shot forward, and he yelled, "Strike two."

The crowd mumbled and muttered, louder this time. In one collective move, people removed fishing caps and sun bonnets, brushing them up and down and fanning themselves. They murmured into the wind. I too removed my cap, scratched the back of my head, and readjusted the brim as I squinted into the sun. I ground my back molars until my jaw ached, willing Woodrow to place a ball short to the outfield so that June could win us the game.

I knew Rufus Steele was directing Woodrow to take those balls, but it was unlikely the next four pitches would be off the mark. Once again, I tried to ignore the comments on the bench, so I missed the time-out call by Dr. Steele. Until, that is, I saw him approach the plate, and put his hand on Woodrow's shoulder. He bent to address Woodrow. They held a brief but earnest conversation. Woodrow nodded twice, turned and re-entered the batter's box.

In a move I had not seen Woodrow make before, he tapped the end of his bat on the far side of the plate, measuring the distance and moving his feet a little. He ignored the catcher's remarks as he ground in the toes of his shoes and spit in the dirt. He choked up on the bat, held it high, stared straight at the pitcher, and got ready for the pitch. Nodding at the catcher's signal, the pitcher wound up and let another fastball fly. The throw was wide of the plate, and I expected Woodrow to let it go. Instead, he made a smooth stride into the ball, connecting with a thundering crack. The ball soared off by itself. The bleacher crowd rose together, stretching up with mouths open, fingers tracking the ball's course as it sailed out to deep center. Four black crows sunning on the outfield fence, climbed suddenly skyward as the ball dropped lazily past them into the branches of the loblolly pines.

A victorious shout erupted from the bench as Woodrow followed Orval and Albert around the bases, lifting his cap and waving gleefully to the crowd as he made his way home with the winning run. He did not run, he flew. On home plate, he firmly pounded both feet and rushed back toward third base to find Rufus Steele. They hugged and slapped and laughed at each other before the pack of admiring fans enveloped them.

I angled through the crowd to join them both. Woodrow wrapped his arms around my chest and bear hugged me so tight I feared he'd break another of my ribs. It was the perfect ending for him, and I reckoned a new beginning as well.

Rufus Steele fixed me with a gaze, a broad smile, and a touch to his gray hat. I wondered again where such a man came from, what he was doing in our small town, and how long he would stay.